"Why ask why I **care?" Amel[ie]** [turned to] **face him. On[ly the slightly]** **slim frame and the hands clenched** **at her sides revealed her tension.**

Lambis didn't answer. To say he cared would be tantamount to inviting them to stay, and that he couldn't do. Yet neither could he see her tension and not respond.

Damn the woman! She'd gotten under his skin once. He couldn't let her do it again.

Suddenly she spun around, and the change in her was a punch to his solar plexus. Gone was the touch-me-not princess, the haughty aristocrat. Everything about Amelie spoke of heat and passion, from her flashing eyes to the flush of color accentuating those high cheekbones and the sweet bow of her mouth, deliciously plump as if she'd been biting it.

The effect was instant and incendiary—a symphony of want turned his body to hot, brazen metal. He'd wanted her before, too many times to count, but not like this—as if he'd incinerate if he didn't reach out and touch her, taste those kissable lips and possess that poised, perfect body.

"My nephew is required to speak. To accept his future role and swear an oath. If he doesn't—" Amelie paused and the color faded from her cheeks "—if he can't say the words, another heir will be found."

"Couldn't the law be changed?"

"Not quickly enough."

The Princess Seductions

Driven by duty—destined for desire!

A dynastic marriage is planned between Princess Amelie of St. Galla and King Alexander of Bengaria. They are meant to be meeting for the first time—but Amelie has disappeared!

Someone must stand in until Amelie returns—and who better than her secret half sister, Cat Dubois?

But when Amelie embarks on a sizzling forbidden affair, will she ever want to return?

Find out what happens in

His Majesty's Temporary Bride

and

The Greek's Forbidden Princess

Both available now!

Annie West

THE GREEK'S FORBIDDEN PRINCESS

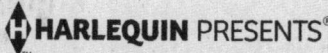

HARLEQUIN PRESENTS®

Recycling programs
for this product may
not exist in your area.

ISBN-13: 978-0-373-21386-3

The Greek's Forbidden Princess

First North American publication 2017

Copyright © 2017 by Annie West

Printed in U.S.A.

Growing up near the beach, **Annie West** spent lots of time observing tall, burnished lifeguards—early research! Now she spends her days fantasizing about gorgeous men and their love lives. Annie has been a reader all her life. She also loves travel, long walks, good company and great food. You can contact her at annie@annie-west.com or via PO Box 1041, Warners Bay, NSW 2282, Australia.

Books by Annie West

Harlequin Presents

The Flaw in Raffaele's Revenge

The Princess Seductions

His Majesty's Temporary Bride

Wedlocked!

The Desert King's Captive Bride

Secret Heirs of Billionaires

The Desert King's Secret Heir

Visit the Author Profile page at Harlequin.com for more titles.

Dedication

For Karen, who's there through thick and thin.
Thanks, mate!

And a big thank you to Efthalia
for advising on the Greek.

Dear Reader,

The Greek's Forbidden Princess is the second book in my The Princess Seductions duet, yet it was the first of the two story ideas that came to me. It's been in my head a long time, slowly percolating till the time was right to get it down in black-and-white.

In my teens I began a love affair with Greece, possibly from the day I picked up a very old edition of stories by Mary Stewart, which featured feisty women finding both peril and romance in the wild mountains of Greece. Strong heroes, passion (if rather understated, keeping with the time they were written) and exotic locations—I was hooked! Since then, I've had the chance to explore a little of the country and its culture, and the fascination continues.

My brooding, powerful hero Lambis, who's cut himself off from the chance of love, owes as much to that early reading as to the traditional *Beauty and the Beast* theme. But the story isn't all about him. In fact, it was Princess Amelie I thought of first. Caring, charming, hardworking and beautiful, she might have been too good to be true except I learned immediately that this woman hides a world of hurt and thwarted hopes behind her serene expression. She loves and cares deeply and would risk anything for those she loves—not only scandal, but heartbreak. So when it's a toss-up between saving her orphaned nephew and begging for help from the man who rejected her...you can imagine what choice she makes!

I felt deeply for Amelie and Lambis. Their story moved me and I hope it moves you, too. I hope, like me, you sigh with pleasure when you reach the final page.

With very best wishes,

Annie

CHAPTER ONE

'THEN KATALEVENO.' I don't understand. Amelie paused and tried again, working to keep her teeth from chattering as the temperature dropped another degree or six. *'Kyrios Evangelos, parakalo.'* Mr Evangelos, please.

The intercom squawked into a burst of machine-gun-fast Greek. Amelie hadn't a hope of understanding. She'd already used up her handful of phrases.

Clearly the woman inside the house had no patience for foreigners. Or language skills other than Greek. Amelie had already tried French, English, German and finally even Spanish and Russian.

But why should the housekeeper, if that was who she was, speak anything other than Greek? This estate was high in the mountain spine of northern Greece. Tourists headed for the beaches of the Aegean Sea or the ancient ruins. Amelie guessed only the most adventurous foreigners headed to this isolated, beautiful region.

Adventurous or desperate.

Amelie had never had a chance to be adventurous. But a twist of fate had turned her staid, predictable world on its head. Desperate was too mild a description for her situation.

'Please. *Parakalo*,' she began, hunching her shoulders against the icy wind, but the line went dead.

Amelie stared, disbelieving, into the security camera perched above the gates. The woman had hung up! She must have seen Amelie shivering in the unseasonable icy blast.

Amelie blinked, torn between indignation and curiosity. This was a first. Never before had she been ignored—no, not ignored…rejected.

Yet even as she thought it, she knew that was wrong.

She'd been rejected by the very man she'd come here to see. Once, when it had been just her happiness in question, she'd taken his rebuff with all the grace she'd spent a lifetime learning. This time, when it was Seb's happiness, his *future* in question, Amelie refused to accept 'no'.

Her mouth settled in a way her father had called obstinate. But her father had never been pleased, no matter how she tried, or how many of the family burdens she shouldered. Besides, he was dead and gone. Like Michel, her brother, and his wife, Irini.

A giant hand gripped her insides and twisted them till they burned. The ache welled high, clogging her chest, her throat, her whole being.

But Amelie wouldn't let it conquer her. She blinked, refusing to let tears come. There'd been no time for tears since the accident for, of course, everyone relied on her to be strong. The burden might have broken her if she hadn't spent years as the anchor for her family and everyone else. For as if grief wasn't enough, the repercussions from Michel's death were...complicated.

Amelie breathed deep, determined to focus on the positive. She still had Seb.

Her glance strayed to the nondescript hire car pulled over in front of the massive gates. There was no movement inside. Seb must still be asleep. Their journey from St Galla had exhausted him.

It had exhausted her. Amelie almost lifted a hand to her aching head—too much stress and too little sleep—but she was conscious of the security camera. She was watched from inside the house she couldn't even see down its long drive.

A lifetime's training in never revealing weakness kept her arm by her side and her chin up. If Lambis Evangelos and his lackeys thought she'd meekly run away...

Her lips turned up in a mirthless smile. They had no idea what despair could do. What *she* could do.

Slowly, shoulders back and hands swinging at her sides, she strolled to the car. She didn't even flinch when the first snowflakes spattered her face.

It needed only that to put the seal on this horrible journey. The secretive trip to Athens on a friend's boat in order to avoid the paparazzi. The press had mobbed her in St Galla and they'd been forced to slip out in the dead of night. The long journey, the crowds and bustle of Athens, then the stonewalling when she'd arrived at the Evangelos Enterprises office. Then the long, exhausting drive north.

She'd come this far. She refused to return home, defeated. There was too much at stake.

Opening the back door of the car, she slid in beside Seb. Sure enough, he was sleeping, a lock of blond hair flopping over his too-pale face. He looked vulnerable, curled up with his teddy under his chin.

Amelie's heart turned over and love, fierce and fortifying, slammed into her. She shrugged out of her long coat and scooted over against him, draping it over the pair of them. He shifted, frowning in his sleep, opening his mouth as if to protest, but then subsided without so much as a whimper. Under the cashmere, Amelie wrapped her arm around him and hugged him close.

They'd hit a dead end and she was out of alternatives. She'd have to come up with another plan, but for now, she'd allow herself a tiny respite. Ten minutes' rest before she revised her plan of action. With a sigh of exhaustion she closed her eyes.

Ten minutes…

A knocking woke her. She had that awful cotton wool taste in her mouth that told her she'd actually fallen asleep in broad daylight.

Except it wasn't daylight. It was murky twilight and so chilly it was a wonder she'd slept.

Again that knocking, harder this time, and Amelie swung her head round. Through the side window she saw a dark shadow loom like a giant mountain bear. Her heart skidded against her ribs. Adrenaline pumped too hard, too fast, and she had to force down a moment's primitive, instinctive fear.

Then she woke properly, remembering their predicament. If only it was merely wildlife she had to worry about!

She slid along the back seat, carefully tucking her coat around Seb, who, remarkably, still slept. The poor kid truly was running on empty.

As she put her hand on the handle, the massive form outside retreated, allowing her to open the door.

Instantly a blast of frigid air struck. Amelie gasped then forced herself out, shutting the door quickly to keep in the relative warmth. Fat snowflakes tickled her face. She sucked in a draught of oxygen that froze her throat and made all the tiny hairs on her body rise.

Except she suspected it wasn't the cold air alone that did that. More likely it was reaction to the great, shaggy bear of a man standing just a pace away.

At least those profoundly broad shoulders blocked some of the wind. They were a perfect frame for a wickedly bold, dark face—straight black eyebrows, strong, too strong nose, high-cut cheekbones and a jaw that reminded her of the Acropolis's uncompromising angles. It didn't matter that his mouth was finely chiselled and full, for he didn't smile. His mouth was grim, a perfect match for eyes as grey and dour as the mountain looming beyond him.

No welcome. No offer of assistance.

Amelie lifted her chin, the better to see him, refusing to be intimidated by that beetling brow or the aggressive bunch of his huge hands.

Or by the unwanted punch of pure feminine response to his aura of potent masculinity.

By sheer force of will she kept her arms at her sides instead of wrapping them around her freezing body. She'd stood firm against the worst St Galla could throw at her, not least her own father. She wasn't about to fall in a heap because of a scowl.

No matter how much she wanted to turn tail and find some cosy hotel where she could curl up and be alone.

This isn't about you, Amelie.

The reminder gave her strength. Her life had always been about others. Her forays into seeking personal happiness had been disastrous.

'Kalimera.' Good day.

He didn't reply. Not by so much as a muscle twitch did his expression change, yet she had the impression that anger coiled tight within that imposing frame.

The only thing about him that moved was his hair, overlong and tousled by the whipping wind, jet black like his eyebrows, and if his expression was any indication, his heart.

How could a man so stern and unyielding make her pulse quicken and her knees go weak with excitement?

'You're blocking the gates.'

Biting back a retort she knew would win her no friends, Amelie smiled. It was the small public smile she sometimes felt she'd perfected before she could walk. The sort that wore well, no matter how tough the circumstances or how much she wished she was anywhere else.

'So I am.' Because parking here had been the only way to guarantee attention. Lambis Evangelos and his employees couldn't drive in or out with her car parked across the entrance. 'If you open the gates I'll remedy that.'

He didn't even bother to shake his head or, being Greek, to lift his chin in that supremely dismissive reverse nod that signified *no*.

Tiredness dragged at Amelie, and a building fury that she'd travelled so far, hiding from the press all the way, fearing someone would recognise them and destroy their anonymity, to be met by *this*. The blank annoyance of a man who didn't give a damn.

Perhaps this last-ditch effort was doomed to fail.

Acid swirled through her insides and the metallic taste of defeat was bitter on her tongue. Amelie felt a tremor of despair begin deep in the pit of her belly and widened her stance, staking her right to be here.

At the movement something flickered in those deep-set eyes, but he said nothing.

So be it. He might be rugged up in a massive coat but Amelie wasn't dressed for this unseasonably early snowstorm. Her clothes were chic rather than warm. The weather on the Mediterranean island of St Galla had been summery. The cool weather wouldn't begin there for another couple of months and snow was rare.

Amelie turned to open the rear car door.

'What are you doing?' His voice was deep and resonant. She felt it circle her ribs then burrow low, making her insides soften.

Suddenly, gloriously, anger welled, burning bright in veins turned sluggish with cold and the prospect of defeat. She would not let this man with a voice like hot whisky, so at odds with those glacial eyes, turn her inside out.

'Since a civil greeting is out of the question, I'm getting back in the car, where at least there's some warmth.'

'Stop.' He stretched out one arm, his big, square hand just a hairsbreadth from hers. Then, abruptly, rejecting the idea of physical contact, he let it drop.

Somehow, more than anything, that hurt.

She didn't *want* him to touch her. But that infinitesimal rejection felt like a tipping point. Amelie assured herself this foolishness was just the aftermath of a hellish time, of stress and trauma and worry.

'Why? Do you have something to say that I want to hear?' Her chin hiked up and to her amazement she caught sight of a tiny twist at the corner of that stern mouth. It was nothing like a smile, nothing so human. But it was *something*.

'You shouldn't be here.'

'This is public property. I've every right to park here while I wait to be let in.'

Those long fingers twitched at his sides and Amelie wondered on a snared breath of icy air whether he fought the impulse to shake her or move her bodily.

'There's nothing for you here.' He said it slowly, enunciating each word with a precise perfection that reminded her English wasn't his native language.

'I didn't come for myself.' Amelie kept her voice even, betraying none of the pain she repressed. She was a master at hiding emotion in public. She did it so well she wondered what it would be like to let go—to cry and complain and rail against the cruelty of fate. But that wasn't her way. She didn't know how.

One sleek eyebrow cocked high in silent interrogation.

'I've brought my nephew.'

Silence. More of that absolute, unnerving stillness. Had he trained in being impenetrable? Or just in being unfeeling?

Surely even this dour man, who'd already made it clear she wasn't welcome, had some kernel of softness for a little boy.

Slowly, as if not trusting her to dash past him and scale the huge gates, he bent and peered into the car. When he straightened his face was unchanged. Clearly little Seb's presence made no difference. They could stay here in what appeared to be a full-scale snowstorm and there'd be no offer of shelter.

Amelie bit the inside of her cheek to prevent the indignant outburst jammed in her mouth.

The sensible thing would be to admit defeat, start the car and drive back to the nearest village, looking for accommodation. She'd do that. Soon.

But her hands shook too much to drive down that winding, slick road. Infuriated, with him and herself, she hauled open the rear door and moved to get in.

Instantly a vice clamped on her shoulder. A hot vice with fingers that dug into her flesh through her thin sweater. His heat after the stinging cold surely explained the rush of energy raying out from the spot.

Amelie turned, meeting that gunmetal stare head-on.

'Don't touch me.'

'Or?' This time both jet-black eyebrows rose.

'Or I'll bring a case of assault so fast your head will spin. And, in case you think I'm bluffing, let me warn you I've reached my limit.'

'Even if it means inviting media attention?'

Because he knew—how could he not?—that she'd only made it this far by avoiding the media.

Carefully Amelie closed the door and turned fully to face him. He was so close he ate up her personal space. He was so big she'd feel crowded and intimidated if she weren't past caring.

'That's one thing about reaching the end of your options. I don't give a damn.' She smiled and this time actually felt pleasure, for she saw the shadow of doubt in his stern face. He'd thought she'd be easier to bully.

'I could call a reporter now. By nightfall we'd have a posse of them here, eager for developments.' Amelie rested her hands on her hips, enjoying the fleeting sense of power that flooded her freezing body.

Yet still he didn't take the bait.

She waited as the seconds ticked into a full minute and more. Still he didn't move or give in.

Even if she followed through and made a formal complaint, or brought in the press, she'd be the one to lose. She and Seb.

They had lost.

She'd gambled against the odds with Seb's future and failed. Now time was running out.

The enormity of it was a body slam, jarring her from head to toe. She had to stiffen her knees to stop from crumpling as she unravelled inside. All her hopes shattered and little Seb... No, she couldn't think about it now, with this man watching her like a bird of prey spying on a mouse. She needed privacy when she finally crashed.

Whiplash fast, she shoved his hand off her shoulder and moved towards the driver's door.

'Where are you going?'

Amelie didn't answer. This was probably the first time in her life she'd ignored a direct question. It should have felt liberating, but all she registered was choking misery.

She ripped open the driver's door. They couldn't stay here. If she was to get them safely back down the mountain they had to go now.

The sound of swearing stopped her. Low and soft, his rich voice turned even the tumble of foreign swear words into a stream of velvet heat.

'Just tell me what you want, Princess.'

Amelie didn't let herself flinch at his bitter use of her title. He said it as if they were strangers. Nor did she turn.

She didn't want to see the steely face of Lambis Evangelos, the man who'd shattered her dreams and now held her hopes for little Seb in his brutally hard palm.

'You.' Her throat closed so it came out as a whisper. She swallowed and tried again. 'I want you.'

CHAPTER TWO

I WANT YOU.

Hell and damnation.

Her words shouldn't have any effect.

They *didn't*. She'd just taken him by surprise. How had she managed it? Where was her retinue of officials and paparazzi?

More important—*why* did she want him?

There was nothing here for her. He'd made that plain three years ago. Besides, Amelie had pride; she wouldn't come after him again.

Lambis scowled. The past was a place he refused to visit.

'You'll need to be more specific. What do you want me for?'

Lambis stared down at her slim form as she slowly turned, her hand white-knuckled on the door, her upswept blonde hair and stunning green eyes the only colour in the scene before him. Her whole body trembled from the wintry blast she refused to acknowledge. She wore pale trousers and a matching sweater that clung elegantly and expensively to her lithe frame but did nothing to keep out the cold.

His instinct on seeing her had been to tear off his coat and wrap it around her slender shoulders.

But he'd resisted. Better to kill her hopes so she left immediately than let her believe she had a chance of staying.

'Seb needs you. As you'd know if you bothered to check my messages.'

Messages he'd left unopened. Returning to St Galla for the funeral had been tougher than even he had imagined. He didn't want reminders of the tragedy and his own guilt. Or of her.

'Seb?' How could the boy possibly need him?

Amelie's mouth flattened. Her eyes had lost their brilliance. They looked opaque with pain, even though her body language was almost aggressive as she leaned into his space. That in itself was remarkable. Amelie was always poised, graceful and polite, the least aggressive person he knew.

Lambis was horrified to realise her eyes looked even more lifeless than on the day they'd buried her brother and sister-in-law. He hated that blankness.

'You haven't forgotten your godson, surely?'

As if on cue Lambis registered movement in the car. A hand palmed the rear window. A pale, tiny hand. Beside it was a sombre young face, golden hair tufted from sleep.

There was no smile of recognition. It was the numbed look of someone who didn't expect a welcome and it cut like a blade to Lambis's belly.

He hunkered beside the door, putting his face on a level with the boy's. Those big eyes regarded him, unblinking. They looked even more desolate than his aunt's, as if they'd never glowed with mischief or delight.

No four-year-old should look that way. But in the circumstances maybe it was inevitable.

Lambis forced his stiff lips into something like a smile. 'Hey, Sébastien. How are you?'

Haunted eyes stared back through the glass. Sébastien said nothing. Nor did his face register emotion. Just that terrible blankness that stirred the frigid waters of Lambis's soul.

Looking at Amelie, and now at Seb, reminded him suddenly of another snowy day on this mountain. The day all the warmth inside him had been snuffed out in a catastrophic blast of icy reality.

Lambis reached for the door, urgently needing to see that little face smile in recognition.

'Don't!' Amelie's voice was sharp as the crack of doom as she inserted herself between Lambis and the car. He found himself staring at a narrow waist and full breasts, her nipples budded enticingly beneath thin wool.

Lambis's breath stalled as heat ignited in his gut. Unseen parts of him might have long since shrivelled and died, but he was still a man, and it had been too long since he'd had a woman.

Through the frosty scent of the thickening snow, he inhaled the gardenia perfume that always made him think of Amelie and sunny St Galla. He remembered how tempting they'd both been. How tough it had been to leave her.

'Why not?' His gaze strayed lower, over the feminine shape revealed by her fitted trousers, and a pulse quickened in his groin. Instantly he rose, shoving his hands in his pockets.

Amelie looked petite and far too fragile, despite the way her chin swung up as if daring him to test her.

'Because I was wrong. I thought you'd help, but the last thing he needs is some fleeting pretend friendly contact with a man who'd bar his door to us. Especially in this.' The tilt of her head indicated the falling snow.

A flake settled on her cheek, melting, but she didn't seem to notice.

'If you'll step away from the car, we'll be on our way.' She folded her arms and her breasts rose, plump and inviting. Lambis yanked his gaze higher.

She wasn't bluffing.

He should be relieved. He didn't have the time or inclination to deal with their problems. He had a multinational business to run, people relying on him. He didn't want Amelie here, stirring emotions, interrupting the smooth running of his life.

Yet he didn't move.

Whatever the problem, Lambis wasn't the man to solve it. He knew his limitations. In his profession it was vital to know your strengths and weaknesses, and those of others. Yet the anxiety he'd felt, seeing Sébastien's staring face, made him hesitate.

She seemed ridiculously dainty to try facing him down. Dainty and shattered, though she tried to hide it.

Snow crunched under his boots as he turned. The gates were high, designed to keep the world out. Yet they swung open at the click of his electronic key.

'You go first. I'll follow you in my vehicle.'

Amelie gripped the wheel too hard as she drove slowly through the dusting of snow.

'Isn't this exciting, Seb? Snow!' Her voice wobbled but she doubted her nephew noticed.

In the rear-view mirror she saw he was at least staring at the view, his expression unreadable. Was he even a tiny bit excited to see snow for the first time? To see Lambis, the man he used to follow like a puppy?

Amelie wrenched her mind to the private road winding around a spur of the mountain.

She couldn't quite believe Lambis had let them enter. If it had been her alone she'd be driving back down to the village now. Lambis didn't want her near. He never had.

Pride smarted at asking for his help. And something else, some tiny part of her that had wondered, even when all hope had fled.

Amelie's breath caught when she saw the house. She'd expected something sleek, hard and impersonal, like Lambis. Instead she discovered a charming traditional mountain house. From the size she guessed it had been significantly extended, but it looked as if the mansion had always sat here, cupped by the mountain on three sides.

The ground floor rose organically from the mountain, its walls of stone. Above that rose another couple of floors, white-finished, and decorated with out-thrust balcony rooms overhanging the walls on wooden struts. They were decorated with intricate wooden carvings. Even the white plasterwork was beautifully decorated with what she guessed were traditional designs. The windows were large and the terracotta roof looked welcoming against the falling snow.

Amelie stopped the car, feeling as if she'd turned a wrong corner. This was the home of megawealthy Lambis Evangelos? The self-contained man who shunned sentiment?

She was staring when her door opened. There he was, his face stern. The wind stirred a glossy black curl at his collar and Amelie wondered what he was like when he relaxed. Once, long ago, she'd seen another side to him, when he was with her sister-in-law, Irini, for the two had been like brother and sister. Occasionally some of that tenderness he kept for Irini had rubbed off and he'd been enough to steal any woman's breath. Especially one who'd been lonely so long.

Amelie blinked and stiffened. She hadn't slept in forty-eight hours. That was why her mind drifted.

'Do you need help?'

She shook her head. 'Seb and I are fine, aren't we, Seb?' She looked in the rear-view mirror and met familiar green eyes. Was he excited? Scared?

Emotion swept through her and she shuddered.

'Amelie?' Lambis's voice was like soft suede on raw skin. It still had the ability to make her *feel*. To *want*.

She felt it now, the buzz of energy in her lower body, the trip of her pulse. Damn! She was past this. She'd moved on, determined not to wallow in regret.

This had to be exhaustion creating phantom emotions.

'Perhaps you could carry the luggage?' She gave him one of her polite smiles, the sort she employed with boring diplomats or boorish industrialists.

For a second that cool stare locked with hers, making her wonder how much he read in her face. Then, with a curt nod, he was gone.

It took no time to bundle up Seb in warm clothes and usher him from the car to the house. Even the crunch of fresh snow beneath his feet barely made him pause and Amelie's heart would have cracked if it weren't already riven. Where was the little boy she'd loved for almost five years? A year ago he'd have been whooping with glee, investigating the unfamiliar icy white.

Now he let her hold his hand. He was wide-eyed but so self-contained it would have scared her if it hadn't become almost normal. She had to find a way to help him.

A sturdy woman with iron-grey hair held the door open, expression inquisitive. This must be the woman who'd cut Amelie off as she'd pleaded to be let in. But, instead of disapproval, Amelie caught shock on the woman's face as she appraised them, then a wide smile of welcome as she scooped Seb in out of the cold and Amelie with him.

'This is Anna, my housekeeper.' Lambis launched into a flurry of Greek that had the woman nodding and smiling. Amelie heard the name Sébastien and her own, then something that made the housekeeper's head jerk up even as she dropped into a curtsey.

'No, please.' Amelie put out her hand in protest. 'Tell her that's not necessary.'

Then the implications of Lambis identifying her sank in. She swung around to find herself facing a massive black-clad chest. She froze, refusing to back up and reveal how daunting it was to be so close to all that brawny strength. His evocative scent, so earthy and male, curled around her.

'There was no need to tell her who I am.'

His eyebrows lifted. 'I respect Anna too much to lie.'

'It's not about lying. It's about revealing only what needs to be revealed.' The memory of the press pack outside the palace gates in St Galla, telephoto lenses trained on the windows and gardens, slammed into her. Bile rose. They'd been eager to snap the grieving Princess or 'the tragic little King', as they dubbed Seb. They'd even tried to bribe the palace employees.

Amelie, who'd lived all her life at the centre of public attention, had never felt so degraded. As if she and Seb weren't real people but sideshow freaks that existed purely for the titillation of the viewing public.

'Can you guarantee your staff won't tell anyone we're here?'

Lambis stiffened. His hard face became unforgiving granite, as if she'd questioned *his* integrity, not raised a valid concern.

'You were the one who arrived uninvited and demanded entry. You'll have to live with the consequences.'

Would Lambis really sell them out to the press? She didn't want to believe it. Once she'd thought she knew him well enough to trust him with her life. But this was Seb's life in question.

'Answer the question, please.'

Lambis folded his arms across that massive chest, like some disapproving god of old passing judgement. It wouldn't surprise her if he suddenly pitched a thunderbolt at her.

'You've had my answer.'

Behind her Anna asked a question and Lambis responded, his tone so brusque and dismissive Seb edged up against Amelie, his teddy squeezed to his chest. Amelie put her hand on his shoulder.

It was the reminder she needed. It didn't matter that she'd once thought Lambis Evangelos had a softer side, or that Irini, her sister-in-law, had said he was the best man alive, apart from her dear Michel. Nor did it matter that he had a reputation for integrity.

Amelie couldn't take risks with her nephew. Despite what she'd threatened outside, Seb needed quiet, not paparazzi camped on the doorstep.

She'd thought they'd be safe with Lambis. He was the CEO of the world's most successful international security firm. His private premises would be more secure, she suspected, even than the St Gallan royal palace. But the consequences if she and Seb had to run the gauntlet of the press whenever they stirred weren't to be borne.

Amelie stroked her nephew's soft hair, bending down as she spoke. 'I'm sorry, *mon lapin*. I made a mistake coming—'

'Don't be absurd! You're not up to driving back down the mountain tonight.' The words were soft but the growl in that bass baritone was unmistakable.

Seb flinched and pressed his face into Amelie's skirt, his arms wrapping round her thighs.

She stood unmoving, shocked by his first overt show of emotion in weeks. Something broke inside her as pity and protectiveness vied with a tiny pulse of hope. Heart welling, Amelie gathered him in. 'It's all right, *mon lapin*. Truly. Everything's going to be fine.'

'Sébastien?' Lambis hunkered in front of the boy but didn't touch. 'I'm sorry. I didn't mean to scare you. I'm not angry, truly. You and your aunt are welcome here.'

Liar. He was furious. But Amelie had no sympathy to spare for the man staring at the little boy with all the wariness of someone facing a man-eating beast.

If the situation weren't so dire she'd almost laugh. As if big, bad Lambis Evangelos, the man who organised protection for the world's most eminent VIPs in some of the most dangerous places in the world, was scared of a child.

'Seb?' Amelie knelt and wrapped him close, inhaling the fresh scents of clean little boy and melted snow. 'Don't be afraid, darling. Everything will be all right. Lambis won't hurt us. In fact—' she lifted her head and glared at the man who hadn't taken his eyes off Seb '—he's sworn to protect you. Did you know that?'

Of course Seb said nothing and Amelie snuggled him tighter, rubbing her hands up and down his thin back.

'Soon we're going to have something to eat

and then I think it will be time for Monsieur Bernhard—'

'Monsieur Bernhard?' Lambis's eyes locked on hers, questioning. She didn't bother to respond. If he couldn't work out that Bernhard was a teddy bear, tough.

'I think he's getting sleepy. It's almost his bedtime. Come on, *mon lapin*, come with Aunt Lili.'

She lifted him in her arms and rose, ignoring Lambis when he made to take Seb.

Did he think she wasn't capable of caring for her nephew? Who did he think had been there through the long nights and lonely days since Michel and Irini died?

Anger threaded the aching grief inside her. Grief for her darling nephew, orphaned so young, and grief for herself.

She saw Lambis move deliberately to block the front door. The obstinate set of his jaw told her it would take a bulldozer to move him.

He didn't want them here. Now he'd decided they couldn't go. She wished he'd make up his mind!

Amelie would walk on hot coals if it would bring back the little boy she adored from the well of shock that had swallowed him. But she was fast running out of strength. Her head was reeling and there was a throb behind her eyes as she fought to stand tall.

Then she felt a touch on her elbow. It was the

housekeeper, Anna, her expression concerned. Gently she raised her hand and stroked Seb's golden hair as he pressed his face into Amelie's collarbone.

'*Ela. Parakalo, ela.*' Come, please come. That much Greek Amelie understood.

She wavered for barely a second. Pride held no place here. She looked at the work-hardened fingers caressing Seb so tenderly and felt the fight drain out of her.

Amelie nodded. '*Efharisto.*' Thank you.

For good or ill they were staying, at least for tonight.

Whether they'd found the safe haven, and the help they needed, only time would tell.

CHAPTER THREE

AMELIE STARED AT the darkness of the swirling night.

She'd got through the last couple of hours like an automaton. At last Seb was tucked up in bed, asleep.

It seemed disloyal to think it—for who could want to see a child in pain?—but surely the way he'd turned to her when they'd arrived, and again when he'd clung to her as she read to him, signified a change? Some lessening of the dreadful nothingness that gripped him?

Rubbing her forehead with weary fingers, Amelie tried to order her fogged thoughts.

She should sleep. She'd eaten the delicious soup and fresh bread Anna had provided, and taken a hot shower in the luxurious bathroom, feeling chilled bones warm.

But she was wired. There was too much to sort out.

Which meant facing Lambis Evangelos.

Sighing, she turned to her suitcase. She wanted to tug on a comfy sleep shirt and pretend she didn't have to face the big, bad wolf tonight. But sleep would elude her till she did.

Ten minutes later, in trousers and a silky shirt

of deep green that matched her eyes and boosted her flagging confidence, she checked that her subtle makeup hid the shadows of fatigue. With a few deft movements she twisted her long hair into a knot. Her earrings were simple pearl studs and she added a fine gold pendant of antique pearls, the only piece of jewellery her mother had given her.

Amelie closed her hand around the pendant, remembering her mother hugging her close, against all royal decorum, and whispering that now Amelie was twelve she was old enough to wear jewellery.

It was a talisman she wore when times got tough. Like when her mother died just months after that twelfth birthday.

Her mother had had the sweetest smile. A smile Michel and his son Seb had inherited. For a moment the ancient image wavered, replaced by Michel's face, the glint in his eyes as he showed off his new speedboat, the charming smile as he invited Irini aboard for a quick spin.

Amelie slammed a steel door on the memory. She snapped open her eyes and deliberately set about cataloguing the beautiful room she'd been given. There was a chance, a slim one, that the place might give a clue to what made Lambis tick, for this was his retreat from the world.

Turning, she saw plain white walls, for the most part bare. Except for a tiny jewel of an icon that glowed richly on the far wall. Amelie wasn't an expert but she recognised it was an original and very, very beautiful. Despite the stiff style of the traditional painting, the serenity and love on Mary's face as she looked down at her baby stole Amelie's breath. Here was love and a joy that made something swell hard in Amelie's chest.

Swiftly she turned away, feeling raw, for she responded to the painting at a visceral level. It tugged at her own secret yearning.

But the important issue was why Lambis secreted this gorgeous piece in a guest room. Why not have it in his room where he'd see it often?

Amelie prowled the space, surveying the high timber ceiling with its ancient beams, the cosiness of intricately woven local rugs on the polished floor and a particularly exquisite one on another wall.

The bed was massive with crisp cotton sheets and a luxurious silk spread. In addition to a huge decorative cupboard was a vast modern walk-in wardrobe. An ancient timber chest carved with mermaids and some mythical beasts she didn't recognise sat under one window, but in a discreet niche was a large screen that swung out to allow guests to watch television from the bed.

The room was an eclectic mix of charming old pieces and sleek functionality. The common thread was money. No expense had been spared to make a guest comfortable.

Which told her what? Lambis valued tradition

but demanded modern convenience? He wanted guests to feel at home?

His reception told her he was more likely to bar the door to guests.

Or perhaps it was just she who was unwelcome.

The idea lodged hard and sharp in her chest. Surely he wasn't so brutal with everyone?

Did he really believe she'd swallowed her pride and come here uninvited because she was needy for *him*?

Nausea snaked through her insides. Of course he had.

And when she'd told him Seb needed him?

He'd still wanted them to leave.

Despite what she'd once thought, the man had no heart. It was as simple as that.

Amelie found him in a sitting room, high-ceilinged and huge. Yet instead of being cold, that signature mix of old beauty and luxurious modern functionality made it feel comfortable.

Until Lambis turned and she read his aloof expression.

There'd been no thawing. Had she really expected it?

Because Anna had fussed over Amelie and little Seb like a hen with a couple of chicks didn't mean the master of the house had changed his mind. Anna's kindness contrasted starkly with Lambis's brooding stare.

He said not a word as Amelie walked the length of the room, to the huge stone-lintelled fireplace with its bright flames and the dark man beside it.

His bold, handsome face was half-shadowed yet unreasonably, appallingly attractive. If you liked remote, harsh beauty. Amelie didn't. Not any more.

Yet her heart skipped as some part that was all instinct and longing, not logic, stirred to life again.

How could he do that to her even now? Anxiety rippled through her. Amelie couldn't let that happen again.

She stopped within the circle of warmth, feeling cold to the bone. The faint scent of fine brandy reached her nostrils and she spied a rounded glass on the mantelpiece. But Lambis didn't think to offer her a drink. Presumably that was too much to expect.

The thought drove thoughts of a conciliatory approach from Amelie's head. If she read him right, she and Seb would be on their way as soon as the snow eased. That would be soon. It was far too early for winter.

Amelie chose a chair by the fire and sank down onto it. She'd fight every step of the way but she was so worn out she'd do it from a position of comfort.

The silence lengthened from seconds to minutes but for once Amelie didn't move to fill it. All her life she'd been the one to charm and please, to smooth ruffled feathers, to be diplomatic and gracious.

She was here to fight for her nephew's future. She wouldn't make small talk, pretending everything was okay.

'Are you going to explain?' he asked finally.

Amelie refused to flinch at that adamantine tone. 'Have you checked the messages I left?'

'I have, but they didn't help. All I know is that this is to do with your nephew.'

Sébastien, she wanted to scream at him. Or *Seb. You've called him both in your time.* Since when had Lambis thought of him only as someone else's nephew?

What had happened to the man who, however reluctantly, had been kind to a little boy who'd shadowed his every move when he stayed at the St Gallan palace? A little boy whose own father was often too busy with affairs of state for a little one to tag along.

'I didn't want to say more until I saw you.' She lifted her chin and met his eyes. In the shadow beyond the fireplace it was hard to read them but they looked shuttered. As if he was determined not to let anyone in. 'It's confidential.'

He lifted one arm in a gesture that encompassed the building. 'There's no one else here but us.'

It was the invitation Amelie needed and yet the words jammed in her throat. She'd hoped for some speck of interest or concern. Was that too much to ask? Instead it was like talking to a stranger.

Surely even a stranger would be more receptive?

Amelie crossed her ankles and folded her hands in her lap, refusing to show hurt. Surely they'd parted friends?

'Seb is adjusting to the loss of his parents.' Not by so much as a tremor did she betray how she too struggled with that tragedy.

Lambis said nothing.

'You saw how he was at the memorial service.' She'd known something was wrong then but it was only since that the enormity of Seb's condition had unfolded.

'He seemed very controlled.'

She shook her head. 'It looked like that. The press *loved* the photos of the brave little Prince saluting his parents' coffins.' Amelie dragged in a hasty breath as pain jabbed her breastbone. The rampant voyeurism of the press had been expected but still it rankled. 'That wasn't control; it was grief.'

Amelie had strenuously opposed taking a four-year-old to the funeral, but though she was now the most senior member of the family she'd been overruled. She wasn't Regent yet, and might never be, if the Prime Minister had his way. St Gallan law still favoured male over female and until Seb was officially proclaimed heir to the throne, and she his Regent, she had no right to make decisions for him.

In fact, she'd broken a slew of laws taking him out of the country. Right now, that was immaterial. The important thing was Seb.

'It hasn't been long since they died.'

Amelie looked into that stern face and saw not a flicker of emotion. Even for Queen Irini, the woman who'd been like a sister to Lambis.

But then, wasn't Amelie too suppressing a riot of pain? It was comforting to think that maybe, somewhere deep behind that inhumanly blank face, Lambis mourned too.

'I know, but…it's more than that.' She paused as a chill of remembrance feathered her spine. No one had expected the King and Queen of St Galla, both in their mid-twenties and full of life, to die in a freak accident. Everyone had been numbed by it. Even now Amelie still woke every morning to that awful reality slamming into her seconds, sometimes whole minutes after she woke.

Amelie held Lambis's gaze. 'Seb saw it happen. He was going to get in the boat too.' She paused and swallowed, the movement scratching a throat suddenly lined with sandpaper. 'But Irini didn't want him too excited before his nap. She handed him to me.' One more deep breath and she went on. 'Michel promised he'd take him for a ride the next day.'

Except there'd been no next day for Michel and his wife.

'I know.' Lambis's deep voice resonated around her, tugging at something sharp and raw inside.

Of course he knew. She'd told him when he'd flown across for the funeral. Why was she going over it again?

Amelie blinked and looked at the fire. It was easier staring at the golden flames than holding his sombre gaze.

'The point is, Seb's reaction to their deaths is… worrying.' She slanted a look at that chiselled face. Still no hint of understanding. 'He hasn't cried. He hasn't spoken. Not since the accident.'

That had Lambis's attention. He stiffened, his brows furrowing down in a V of concentration, or could it be concern?

'Hasn't spoken at all?'

'Not a word. Not to anyone.'

It had been uncanny, the way little Seb had stayed silent through those first days. It had worried her then but there'd been so much to attend to, so many legal matters and royal duties, meetings and consultations, she'd let herself hope she was wrong and it would resolve itself.

'He doesn't talk or smile or cry. He doesn't *react*.' Just saying it sent a quiver through her. She'd never felt so helpless.

'You've sought advice?'

'Of course. The consensus is that he needs time,

though no one knows how much. Time and to feel safe and loved.' Her voice caught on the last word but she refused to look away. She wasn't ashamed of her feelings for Seb.

It was only what she'd once felt for Lambis that embarrassed her.

'Then give him time. Give him love. Be patient.'

It was what the experts had said, each of them studiously ignoring the flaw in that simple approach.

'I can't.'

'What do you mean, you can't?' Lambis had never thought to hear such words from Amelie. They shocked him more than if she'd begun unbuttoning that slinky shirt and invited him to make free with that delectable body.

He scowled furiously.

He didn't want her here.

He didn't want to get involved.

The fact his mind couldn't stop conjuring images of a sexy, pouting princess, eager for his touch, was flame to the last shreds of his patience.

'Of course you can. It's what you *do*!'

Despite her regal posture and renowned diplomatic skills, the woman was a walking advertisement for all those soft, feminine emotions. She'd raised her younger sibling after her mother's death, since their father, more concerned with power and his own pleasure, had no interest in family life. She'd been the stable, loving centre of their family.

She'd warmly welcomed Irini, married at twenty and feeling out of her depth in royal red tape and a new country.

Lambis still had the letters full of Irini's eager confidences. About how caring Amelie was. How easy to talk to. When others counselled against a royal marriage simply for the sake of an unborn child, Amelie had taken the young lovers' cause and won the day.

For that alone he owed Amelie a debt.

He watched her stiffen, her spine so straight you could use it as a ruler. 'It may be what I *do*, as you so dismissively put it, but I can't this time.'

Lambis opened his mouth to explain he wasn't being dismissive, then caught himself. Never explain. Never discuss emotions. From a safe distance he might admire Amelie's loving nature and the way she shared herself with her family as well as her nation, but it wasn't his way.

Not any more.

Now her hackles were up. He watched, fascinated and, yes, relieved, as colour tinted her too-pale face. Princess Amelie of St Galla was a stunning woman. The warmth of her personality had a way of insidiously wrapping itself around your insides till you could almost believe...

'You can't? Why not?' His voice sounded as if

it scraped over ground glass. Not surprising when his throat felt coated with shards.

'It means, much as I want to, I won't have a chance. Time's running out for Sébastien and we can't afford to wait for time to heal him. Besides—' she averted her eyes to stare into the fire '—the palace is no place for him to recuperate. Everywhere he turns there are memories of his parents. He only has to look from his window to see the bay where they died.'

He heard it now, the faintest tremor in her voice. Behind the faultless display of calm, Amelie was hurting.

Once Lambis would have gone to her and—

What? Put his hand on her shoulder? Cuddled her close? Assured her everything would be okay?

He couldn't do it. Not least because he knew touching this woman would be the biggest mistake of the decade. There was no knowing where he'd stop once he started.

More importantly, Lambis no longer believed in happy endings.

He couldn't lie to her. He'd never been able to do that, though for a while he'd been tempted. When, years before, she'd looked at him with those beautiful, luminous eyes and suggested he might spend more time in St Galla, not for Irini's sake, but for hers. He'd been tempted to let her believe he could be the man she wanted, just to bask in her adoration.

'Then take him somewhere quiet. Somewhere he can rest.'

Her eyes met his and fire flashed in his blood. 'Easier said than done. Everywhere we go are reporters.'

'Yet I didn't see the paparazzi outside my gates.' The more he thought about it, the more remarkable it was. He, with his experience as a bodyguard and later, running the best of the best in close personal protection, knew how difficult it was for non-professionals to evade a determined press. Yet Amelie had brought her nephew from St Galla, an island near the coast of France and Italy, all the way to Greece without being followed.

How had she managed it? He wouldn't have thought it possible for a woman who'd led a sheltered life behind palace walls.

'For now.' Her tone, like her face, was stony. 'You know I can't evade them long-term. We need somewhere safe and secure.'

Somewhere like this.

'This is my home, not a safe haven.' Not for anyone but himself.

'You promised to protect Seb. I heard you tell Irini when she asked you to be his godfather.'

The mention of Irini was a lead weight dragging at his guilty conscience. Another life he'd failed to protect.

'I'll find you both a place you can hide away

from the press till you return to St Galla. Somewhere suitable.'

Somewhere not here.

Amelie regarded him coolly. She didn't raise an eyebrow or twitch a muscle, yet she made it clear his answer wasn't enough. For the first time in their personal interactions she turned into Princess Amelie. A woman who held her own with heads of state and tough negotiators. A woman with generations of blue blood in her veins. A woman prepared to take him on in his own territory.

No one did that. For years now Lambis had given orders and they'd been obeyed. His advice was highly sought, his presence ditto.

Yet Amelie's cool regard told him she expected more.

'So you'll find your godson a bolt-hole then wash your hands of him?'

Her words pierced his conscience. Or maybe it was what remained of his heart.

'It's for the best.'

She shook her head. 'I truly believed you cared. I thought you a man of honour.'

She rose. His trained eye noticed the slight wobble in her legs. She fought emotion or exhaustion or both, determined not to let him see.

She was so valiant his respect for her soared. Even as he wished her and her demands to the very devil. For she was wrong. He wasn't the man to help. He wasn't the man she believed.

She spun on one heel, walking away.

It was what he wanted. Yet his gut hollowed.

'You said time's running out.' The words jerked out before he was conscious of forming them. 'What did you mean?'

'Why ask when clearly you don't care?' She didn't even turn to face him. Only the rigidity of her slim frame and the hands clenched at her sides revealed her tension.

Lambis didn't answer. To say he cared would be tantamount to inviting them to stay, and that he couldn't do. Yet nor could he see her tension and not respond.

Damn the woman! She'd got under his skin once. He couldn't let her do it again.

Suddenly she spun round and the change in her was a punch to the solar plexus. Gone was the touch-me-not Princess, the haughty aristocrat. Everything about Amelie spoke of heat and passion. From her flashing eyes to the heightened colour accentuating those high cheekbones and the sweet bow of her mouth, deliciously plump as if she'd been biting it.

The effect was instant and incendiary—a symphony of want turned his body to hot, brazen metal. He'd wanted her before, too many times to count, but not like this—as if he'd incinerate if he didn't reach out and touch her, taste those kissable lips and possess that poised, perfect body.

Her chin tilted as if she read his lust and was

disgusted by it. Yet when she spoke Lambis realised she'd noticed nothing but the worries tormenting her.

'Because he's underage, Seb can't be crowned King. Instead he'll be officially proclaimed heir and a regent will be confirmed. The date for the proclamation ceremony has been set for his fifth birthday next month. Since he's no longer an infant, on that day he must personally accept his new status.'

'And?'

'And he's required to speak. To accept his future role and swear an oath. If he doesn't—' Amelie paused and the colour faded from her cheeks '—if he can't say the words, another heir will be found.'

'But in the circumstances—?'

Amelie's mouth thinned. 'The law of succession is specific. He must make the oath himself or be barred from the throne for ever.'

Lambis felt his brow furrow. 'But he's Michel and Irini's only son.'

'And the throne is his birthright. But that doesn't matter. What matters under St Gallan law is establishing the next ruler as soon as possible. If it's not Seb then I'm informed it will be a distant cousin, a man currently being investigated for fraud.'

Her words fell like blows. Irini's son disinherited? It didn't seem possible.

'Couldn't the law be changed?'

'Not quickly enough for Seb.'

'What about you?' When she simply stared he continued. 'Why not make you Queen if the next legitimate heir is so distant?' After all, she'd carried much of the royal burden, both for her father, then later for her younger brother as he'd adapted to the role of King.

'Women don't inherit the St Gallan throne. That's a male privilege.' Her tone was dispassionate, but Lambis wondered what it was like, eldest child of a monarch, forced to make a career out of diplomacy and public service, knowing you were barred from taking the throne for ever.

'I need to help Seb find his voice again, because that will mean he's recovering. *And* because without it he'll be denied what should rightfully be his.' She wrapped her arms around herself and something clenched in Lambis's chest. It was so rare for Amelie to reveal vulnerability. 'I couldn't live with myself knowing I'd failed Michel and Irini's trust in me.'

Lambis reached for the brandy he'd nursed before she arrived. One swallow and it shot a heated trail through his chest and down to his belly.

Amelie's talk of trust evoked the harsh remembrance of his responsibility to Irini. Lambis had failed his friend once, with dire consequences. If he failed her son…

'Why bring him here? I'm not a psychologist or speech therapist.'

Her face changed at his words. The grimness turning down her mouth at the corners eased, as if she sensed him weakening.

'He's fascinated by you. You know how he followed you around every time you came to visit. He thinks the world of you.'

Her shoulders lifted in the smallest of shrugs as if she couldn't fathom her nephew's taste. Nor could Lambis.

'I couldn't think of anyone else he cared about so much that they might help him through this.'

Lambis shook his head so vehemently he felt the tickle of his hair on his neck and jaw.

'I wouldn't have the first idea how to help him.'

But that wasn't what made Lambis's chest ice over. It was the idea of anyone, especially that small boy, depending on him to save them.

What a fraud he was! Every day he managed arrangements to protect strangers, some of them in the most fraught environments, but he couldn't protect those closest to him.

It was a cosmic joke. And the tragedy of it was it was no joke. It was all too real.

The consequences haunted him every day.

He looked back to find her eyes fixed on him as if trying to see into his soul. He wished her luck with that. He was pretty sure he no longer possessed one.

Carefully he put the empty glass on the mantelpiece. 'I can't do what you want.'

'You won't try?' Her fine features paled, pared back by tension and disappointment.

'I'm not the man to help Seb. I'm sorry.'

He thought her mouth would crumple, and pain, swift and sharp as a javelin, lanced his chest.

'Then God help him.' She swung around and strode away, heels clicking on the polished floor.

'I'll find a retreat for you both. Somewhere the press can't bother you.' It was the best he could do. His pride and his conscience howled that it was far too little. But he refused to raise false hope. He was no miracle worker. Better for Seb to spend quiet time with his aunt. Surely that was all the miracle he needed. 'It will be sorted by tomorrow.'

Amelie didn't even pause on her way out of the door.

CHAPTER FOUR

LAMBIS TURNED FROM his computer, catching sight of figures outside.

Amelie and Sébastien, out so early that the snowy peak rising behind them glowed pink and orange.

Intrigued, he shoved his chair from the desk and moved to the window. They were an unlikely pair. The Princess wore waterproof boots that were too big for her and a bulky waterproof jacket he guessed was Anna's. Seb's clothes fitted better but the jacket was too long. Where had Anna found the gear?

Amelie led the boy across the pristine white of last night's fall. Maybe they were out early because she knew the snow wouldn't last. By this afternoon it would have disappeared. The forecast was for a return to warm weather. Not that they'd be here then.

He needed to get back to his messages. But he stayed where he was, watching.

Amelie talked, waving her arm enthusiastically. Seb said nothing and, though he walked beside her, his shoulders were slumped and his head drooped. He didn't act like a kid enjoying the first snow of the season. No bounding across the white to leave footprints. He didn't even bend to make a snowball, much less attempt a snowman.

As if reading Lambis's thoughts, Amelie dropped to her knees and began scooping the white stuff together in a mound. Her face, pink with cold, was breath-stealingly beautiful. She smiled, talking as she worked, but there was a quality about her smile that spoke of strain.

She gestured, inviting the boy to join in, but he simply stood and watched.

The Princess's expression froze for a second before she ducked her head, ostensibly concentrating on her task. When she looked up again her smile was as bright as ever.

Yet Lambis *felt* her pain. His chest clenched around the hurt. She was so stoic, so determined to persevere, even against what looked like hopeless odds.

Her words last evening had kept him awake all night, trying to fathom a way to help them. To help Irini's child. To ensure Seb wasn't deprived of his inheritance.

Lambis didn't have what it took to get through to the boy. All he could do was lavish money on the problem and bring in the best specialists. But she'd already done that.

Which left him helpless and useless.

Lambis folded his arms across his chest, feeling the thunderous crash of his heart against his ribs. Frustration rose.

But that had always been his problem, hadn't it?

He could look out for himself, he could keep total strangers safe but when it came to those close to him...

A shuddering breath seared his lungs as he fought the gathering blackness.

Outside in the bright light Amelie hid her fear behind that glorious smile.

As Lambis watched, something twisted and broke inside. His breath expelled in a huge rush and he found himself striding for the door.

'When we're done we'll ask Anna if we can have a carrot for his nose. What do you think?'

Of course, Seb said nothing and Amelie was left to pretend she was having the time of her life, kneeling in the snow while her heart broke a little more.

She'd spent her life hiding feelings behind a charming smile but this was harder than anything she'd ever done. Each day, each hour, was more difficult than the last. She feared soon she wouldn't be able to do it any more. But if she couldn't be strong and reassuring for Seb, who would?

Movement caught her eye. It was Lambis, immensely tall and broad-shouldered, rounding the corner of the house. He wore boots, a black pullover and black jeans. With the golden light catching his bold, unsmiling features, he could have been the god of the mountain, marching down to see who'd invaded his territory.

Amelie's heart gave a little leap and she looked away, concentrating on getting more snow for her rather pathetic snowman.

One day she wouldn't feel this automatic spark of attraction, the infinitesimal catch to her breath when she saw him.

That day couldn't come soon enough.

When she looked up Lambis had stopped. His attention wasn't on her, but on Seb, and there was something about that hard, handsome face that made her still.

It wasn't brooding anger or disapproval. It looked like desolation.

Amelie recognised it because it was how she'd felt when her mother died, and again after losing Michel and Irini. And this morning, waking to the knowledge there was no one to help her help Seb. That the chance of bringing him back from wherever he was, in time for the royal proclamation ceremony, was almost nil.

She looked at Lambis's still face and fought to make sense of what she saw. He looked...haunted, his mouth a twist that tugged at something deep within.

Instinct urged her to go to him and find out what had triggered his anguish. To comfort him. But the memory of his words last night stopped her.

It's what you do! That was what he'd said.

It was true. She was a nurturer, a carer, yet he'd made it sound like a terrible weakness.

She'd do anything for the people she loved. She'd supported her family and her people all her life. She believed in love. Yet the only times she'd reached out for love, she'd been rejected. Years ago the man she'd wanted to marry had abandoned her, frightened off by her father. The second time it had been this man, Lambis Evangelos, telling her he wanted nothing to do with her.

Well, he could whistle for sympathy. She was *not* wasting her emotions on him!

'A snowman, eh? Not a bad effort considering there's very little snow.' His voice startled her. It held a hint of warmth that reminded her of the man she'd once believed she'd known, years ago in St Galla.

Amelie sucked in a breath of frigid air and let it out as Lambis hunkered beside her and added a clump of snow to her lopsided construction.

'You're out of practice, Princess. Obviously you don't get enough snow on St Galla.' He glanced at Seb, drawing him silently into the conversation, but didn't wait for a response. Instead he reached out his long arms and gathered more snow in one scoop than she'd managed in four, adding it to the now rotund snowman.

And just like that the pent-up fury inside Amelie dissipated.

She couldn't forgive Lambis his refusal to help.

But for this moment he was an ally. For a few precious moments, she felt a weight lift from her shoulders as Lambis talked about the deep snows of winter. Lambis, the man who could be taciturn to the point of absolute silence.

Amelie sank back on her heels, brushing back a stray strand of hair with a horribly shaky hand. This morning she'd felt alarmingly close to breaking point, her emotions too near the surface. For weeks there'd been no one to share her worries about Seb except Enide, the elderly cousin who'd moved into the palace to support them when Michel and Irini died.

Dear Enide. She was the only one Amelie had trusted with the truth about this trip, though Enide didn't know exactly where Amelie was so she didn't have to lie if questioned. She was back in St Galla holding the fort, presiding over the few minor royal events that couldn't be cancelled while Amelie and Seb took their 'private holiday'. The major event, a gala celebration with the King of Bengaria, was being rescheduled to next month.

'There, that's better.'

Amelie watched in amazement as Lambis plucked two pebbles from the ground, uncovered by their scrapings, and pressed them into the snowman's face, creating eyes.

Was this the same man who'd rejected her and Seb last night?

'Very fetching,' she murmured.

She glanced at her nephew. His attention was on the little, icy man they'd made. But there was no glow of appreciation or even interest in his expression. Just that blankness that terrified her.

Beside her Lambis rose to his vast, imposing height in one quick movement and Seb started. He didn't precisely shrink back, but he stiffened. So did Lambis. Amelie felt the tension in his big frame, felt it in his utter stillness. Seb was nervous of Lambis, but Lambis was just as wary of him.

What had she expected? That Lambis would bond with the boy over a game in the snow and change his mind about helping?

Grumpy with herself because that was exactly what she'd hoped, Amelie got to her feet and shepherded Seb towards the house.

'Come on, Seb. It's breakfast time. I'm sure Anna's got something nice for us to eat.'

Lambis's voice followed them. 'Then you can pack. I've organised a place for you to stay where you'll be comfortable and private. Somewhere less wintry.'

He couldn't wait to be rid of them, could he?

Amelie halted, hackles rising despite her attempt to stay calm. But it seemed she'd shed that ability last night.

What was it about Lambis Evangelos that made her feel so *different*? Unlike the controlled, careful woman she'd been for twenty-nine years? Every fine hair on her arms and the back of her neck prickled.

The man was immovable. She should walk away, not let him see how his rejection hurt.

Instead, Amelie discovered she really *had* reached breaking point. There was no other explanation for the instinct that made her, quick as thought, bend and scoop up a handful of snow. She packed it into a hard ball, then spun round and lobbed it straight at the tall figure behind her.

For the first time she could recall, Amelie had no thought for good manners or appropriate royal behaviour—things that had been drummed into her from birth. Only for the need to wipe the satisfaction off her tormentor's face.

Snow exploded on his chin, showering him in white.

For a second, not quite believing she'd done it, Amelie stared, her eyes widening. Then, as he spat out snow, she couldn't prevent the laugh that bubbled up and escaped her frozen lips. A laugh of shock and delight. If she'd aimed properly she couldn't have done better. He looked as astonished as her.

Amazing how good that felt!

To act recklessly. To attack instead of taking her disappointment like a proper princess, always gracious and polite.

Amelie felt a rogue ripple of power through her

chest and right down her spine. After the tension and worry of the last weeks it was marvellous.

She was still smiling when Lambis bent, shovelling up a massive handful of snow, shaping and throwing it all in one fluid movement.

It thudded into her arm, raised protectively in front of her face. Without stopping to consider where this would lead, Amelie scrabbled up another handful of snow, compacting it. She pitched it just as another massive snowball hit her shoulder, disintegrating in a starburst of white that blurred her vision.

Amelie couldn't catch her breath. It came in choppy little gasps of searing cold as she bent and reached for more snow. It took a second to realise it was laughter choking her airways, a hoarse chuckle that melded amusement with the rush of pent-up emotions, suddenly let loose. Her pulse was hectic, out of control, and satisfaction sung in her veins as she got Lambis square on the chest, white slamming into his black pullover.

Then his lob caught her full on the face.

The shock of it made her wobble in her borrowed boots, breathing in snow crystals.

When she swiped her face clear it was to see Lambis, arrested in mid movement, watching to see if she'd faint or curse or run away. As if!

Amelie dived for the snow, using two hands to make a massive snowball. 'You may be quick, Evangelos, but you're a much bigger target.' This time her aim was off, catching him on the elbow as he moved, but the joy of a hit urged her on. Ignoring the pelt of snow on her shoulders and chest, she took her time with the next, catching him on the neck as he twisted away.

The woman was utterly glorious.

Gone was the pale, serious Princess who'd twisted his conscience and his belly in knots last night. Instead Amelie glowed. From her bright blonde hair, escaping in loose tendrils around her face, to her incandescent smile and the vivid green of her eyes. Even with snow dripping down one cheek and wetting her hair, she was more beautiful, more vibrant than anyone he'd ever seen.

Lambis wanted to reach out and capture the essence of her.

He wanted to turn his back and run from her.

And keep running.

Because no good could come from this.

Damn. She turned him inside out! Every time he pushed her away she sneaked under his guard. And she didn't have a clue she did it. She brimmed with a joy that was artless and contagious. He could almost feel his lips twitch in response and—

Ice exploded on his face. Lambis brushed it off and shook his head, shaking snow crystals from his hair. That was when he noticed Sébastien, tucked up against the corner of the house, watching. His features were as blank and unsmiling as before. But Lambis saw his eyes looked different...engaged.

Memory stirred, of that same little boy skipping along beside him in St Galla, chattering about everything and nothing, asking so many questions his head spun, laughing at some absurd rhyming game he'd made up.

Heat stabbed. Lambis had tried in the past to avoid Sébastien but it hadn't worked. In the end he'd almost become accustomed to having the kid as his shadow. Now, seeing that glimmer of animation in his eyes brought memories flooding. Memories he'd repressed.

Amelie caught him staring and turned too. She stilled then swallowed hard, her gaze on her nephew. Yet she didn't go to the boy. Instead she quickly turned back, scooping up more snow as if she hadn't noticed the change in Sébastien. But she had. It was there in her too tight mouth and the sudden, rapid blink of her eyes.

She was scared, he realised. Distress clawed his vitals. Scared that by going to Sébastien, by making a fuss, the child would retreat again into complete blankness.

That was the moment, as her next missile hit him full on the chest, Lambis decided, against every instinct for self-preservation, he'd travel with them to the refuge he'd organised.

He raised both hands in surrender. 'Enough. We

need to get dry and you two need to eat. You've got a long trip.'

Immediately Amelie stilled. Though she kept her chin up and her shoulders straight, he sensed strain behind her calm façade. Because he'd already glimpsed her pain?

Lambis discovered he preferred her defiance, even the contempt she'd shown last night, than this careful nothingness that uncannily resembled her nephew's expression.

'I hope you like flying, Sébastien.' It was the first time he'd addressed the child directly since they'd arrived, but it was easier now than addressing his aunt. 'I'm taking you in a helicopter and the view from up there is terrific. You can see all the villages and the winding mountain roads. It's almost like looking at a map.'

'*You're* taking us?' Amelie's brow wrinkled.

'Don't worry. I'm a qualified pilot. It's the fastest option, and the least public.' He watched her digest that. 'I'll have someone return your hire car.'

If he'd expected thanks he'd have been disappointed. Amelie merely nodded and took Sébastien's hand, drawing him towards the house.

Lambis took his time following. His plan had been to have someone else escort them to his island villa in the Ionian Sea to the west of the mainland. It was a simple arrangement and it had the beauty of removing his unwanted guests as soon as possible.

Yet he'd changed his plans. All because of the jagged hurt when he saw Irini's little boy bereft and Amelie so heartbreakingly stoic.

Which was inexplicable since Lambis no longer had a heart to break.

CHAPTER FIVE

AMELIE HAD SEEN a lot of beautiful things. From the royal heirloom jewellery she'd inherited, to the view from the palace of St Galla across the Mediterranean. From ballrooms and exquisite finery to the joy on her sister-in-law Irini's face the day Seb was born.

Yet she caught her breath as Lambis brought the helicopter towards a small island ringed by azure and turquoise water. Pale cliffs cupped sheltered, secret coves and elsewhere the rocky, wooded slopes eased down to beaches so white they could have been spun from sugar.

Winter was a lifetime away from this place, basking in bright sunlight. In the distance she spied a small village curved around a tiny natural harbour, but her attention focused on the house that stood alone on this side of the island. A rambling house that seemed to grow from the rocks and flow down the hill towards its private, pristine beach.

'Your place?' she asked through the microphone on her headset. How else could he arrange so quickly a hideaway for them, safe from the prying press?

'Yes.' He paused then added, 'It's only just finished.'

Amelie swung round to watch Lambis as he brought the chopper down onto a helipad tucked behind the house. It was a tiny thing but the added information about the house being new was unnecessary. Last night, when they'd arrived at his mountain home, there had been no unnecessary words from him.

Did this signify a softening? Like the way he'd been in the snow this morning? Or was she seeking signs of a thaw because she so desperately wanted them?

She turned back to Seb. 'Do you see the pretty colour of the water and the white beaches? It's probably still warm enough to swim here.'

'It is.' Again that bass baritone filled her ears. 'The snow in the mountains was unseasonably early. Winter won't reach here for months.'

Amelie smiled at Seb, helping him with his seat belt, trying to still the hope clamouring inside. Lambis had decided to help Seb recover after all. She couldn't stop the optimistic quickening of her heart.

'The staff here will look after you both. Anything you want, just ask them.' He didn't even look at her, instead concentrating on the control panel as the rotors slowed. 'The place is yours for as long as you need it and there will be no press intrusion.'

What thanks she might have offered dried and crumbled in her throat. So, they were to be left with the staff, not their host. Amelie firmed her mouth and helped Seb out of his headphones, hanging them up then taking hers off. Of course she was grateful Lambis was providing a refuge but she'd actually believed he'd changed his mind.

Appalling how much it hurt to realise she'd been wrong. How many more times would she let this man hurt her?

The door opened and Lambis was there already, holding it open, eager for them to go. She lifted Seb out, not trusting herself to look at Lambis. But his tall, intimidating presence made every sense prickle. Her reaction was pure disapproval, like a spitting cat's fur standing on end. It could *not* be sexual awareness. That would be the ultimate self-betrayal.

A woman on the edge of the helipad smiled and approached, introducing herself as the house-keeper, welcoming them.

It was so civilised, so *easy*. Lambis would remove them from his presence with as little fuss as if he'd ordered a meal.

Fury, hurt, grief, and all the despair she'd battled for so long rose like a column of fire, filling her till Amelie felt as if she were about to explode.

She smiled at the housekeeper, though it hurt her frozen facial muscles, and asked her to take Seb ahead while she, Amelie, had a quick word with Lambis. The fact Seb went with the woman, without hesitation or a backward look, simply compounded her incendiary emotions.

Once he'd have either skipped ahead, eager to explore, or, if tired, hung back, clutching her hand. Every day the change in him tore at her heart, and her sense of helplessness grew.

She watched them head to the house, all the while aware of Lambis standing like an enormous, encompassing shadow behind her. She never needed to see him to know where he was. Right from the first time he'd come to St Galla for Michel and Irini's wedding, Amelie had been able to pinpoint his location with unerring accuracy. There was a little buzz of awareness whenever he was around, a preternatural sense that never failed.

How shaming that even after he'd rejected her she was still attuned to him!

She swung round. He was too close. She had to lift her head to meet his eyes.

'What sort of man are you?'

His brows drew together in a frown, yet even that didn't detract from the powerful attractiveness of those bold features. Amelie's heart rapped hard and fast and she knew it was only partly from anger.

Her green eyes sparked and Lambis felt an answering flare deep in his belly. The Amelie he'd known was charming, attractive, delightful, but never confrontational. Not till she'd arrived at his Greek home. Perversely, he found her vibrancy, the raw energy of her emotions, arousing.

'Have you no heart?' Her finger jammed into his breastbone, right where his heart pumped too hard, too fast. He tried to tell himself it was because no one else would dare speak to him like this, but he knew it was from the effort of not sweeping her into his arms and kissing her into silence.

It had been there inside him ever since she'd turned up on his doorstep—the clawing hunger that grew more voracious each time they met. That sense he could cheerfully lose himself in this woman and never surface again.

It was outrageous and horrifying, for she could never be for him. He'd taken pains to sever his links with her.

Yet he'd spent untold nights sleepless, wondering how Amelie's lips tasted. How it would feel to meld his body with hers. Seeing her in the snow this morning, so outwardly cheerful, yet, he sensed, so close to the brink of emotional collapse, had punched a hole through the wall he'd built around himself. A hole he couldn't mend, no matter how often he reminded himself he was no saviour, either for the boy or her.

'Did you hear me?' She looked outraged and delectable.

'I heard, Princess.' He captured that jabbing hand, encircling it with his, drawing it down to their side. She was warm and smooth, her flesh soft against his calluses. Even that simple touch seemed erotically charged. At least to him.

Clearly she didn't notice.

'And you have nothing to say?' Indignation coloured her tone. 'You really are some piece of work.' She shook her head. 'To think Irini loved you. She said you were the brother she'd never had. She said she'd trust you with her life.'

A great tremor of pain started somewhere in Lambis's belly and rose, spreading everywhere. Irini had trusted him and he'd let her down.

'What's wrong?' Amelie's words were machine gun fire, aimed at his heart. 'You don't like to be reminded that Irini would expect you to do more for Seb than fob him off?'

'I'm not fobbing him off.' The words ground from him. Hadn't he brought them here? Wasn't he doing his best to protect them?

'You're deserting him. Because you can't be bothered to give up your precious time.' The words peppered him. 'Or...' she tilted her head to survey him '...because you're afraid.'

Lambis stiffened, stunned. How did she know? He hadn't even admitted it to himself. But she was right, he realised in shock. He was scared at a bone-deep level he couldn't explain to anyone, especially this bright, brave woman who stared at him with such contempt.

'I can't imagine what your problem is, Lambis. I don't want to know. But you're not the man I thought. Or the man Irini believed you. I don't know how you can live with yourself.'

Lambis didn't respond as the missile words slammed into him. They weren't anything he hadn't told himself. Yet, hearing them from Amelie, he felt himself dredge a new low.

But it was nothing to the ragged, raw pain that seared him when he saw her eyes turn over-bright with unshed tears.

'Don't, Amelie!' With one urgent movement he tugged her to him so hard he heard the soft huff of her breath as she landed on his chest. He wrapped his arms around her, pinioning her so she couldn't move, pressing her face into the place where his heart thudded like an out of control piston.

His breath sawed through cramped lungs. The whole of him hurt, except where he touched Amelie. For they fitted together perfectly, her head tucked under his chin, her feminine softness balm to his rigid body. It was all he could do not to stroke her, soften his hold and explore that lithe body.

Did she feel it too? The rising need? She didn't struggle to pull back.

Who was he kidding? She despised him. Whatever feelings she'd once had for him were dead and buried, and who could blame her?

How he'd had the willpower three years ago to resist her overtures and draw back from her he didn't know. But then he'd never held her in his arms, had he? He'd had that much honour at least, even though the temptation to hold her, to have her, had been almost impossible to resist.

Just as the need to lift her chin now and taste her lips was a compulsion he needed all his strength to fight.

With a mighty effort he lifted one hand, intending to let her go. Instead he watched his fingers stroke the wheaten ripeness of her hair. His breath shuddered at how soft it was, so at odds with the severely simple way she'd styled it high on her head.

Lambis drew in a deep breath that brought with it the scent of gardenias. He bent his head, burying his face in her hair. It was like diving into silken sunshine richly perfumed with flowers. For a second longer he stood, indulging the craving he'd managed to withstand for so long.

Then he dropped his hands and stepped back.

Amelie's eyes were enormous, the irises wide as if she'd just woken. Her trembling fury was gone. Instead she looked stunned, just as he felt. But of course that was his imagination working overtime. Amelie hated him. She no longer cared for him. He should be glad. He didn't want her to care, did he? He'd gone to great lengths to ensure she didn't.

'You're wrong, Amelie. I'm not the one Sébastien needs. I can't help him talk again.' He wished he could. It would be some small salve to his conscience. 'But I'll stay.' For her sake. Because it scared him to see this poised, generous woman distraught.

'You'll stay?' Her whisper skated across his

senses. Even now, seeing her distressed, he had to fight his baser male instinct to haul her in and kiss her into oblivion. Or preferably into his bed.

Lambis raked a hand through his hair. This was a mistake; he knew it with every fibre of his being. With the sixth sense he'd honed in years of protection work. But he couldn't walk away.

'I'll stay. But don't expect a miracle. The boy's scared of me, if anything.' The way Sébastien had cringed last night when Lambis had growled his displeasure haunted his conscience. 'And I have a business to run. I'll be in my office most of the time.'

But Amelie was nodding, her mouth turning up into a tentative smile of hope that caught him in the chest.

'Thank you, Lambis. I...' She shook her head as if speaking was too hard and again he felt that terrible plummeting sensation. She wasn't listening. She was building hopes that were doomed to be smashed. 'This means so much.'

He couldn't bear the gratitude in her voice or the hope in her eyes. He turned towards the house. 'Just put it down to my one act of generosity for the decade.'

Next morning the sun shone bright and clear, sparkling off the vast infinity pool that encircled the front of the house, and the turquoise waters of the sea beyond.

Amelie felt the heat on her arms as she stood, enraptured. In St Galla the palace sat high on its headland, looking across gardens and forest to its private cove. She'd always loved the view. But this was something else. They were right down near the shore, as if the house were part of the landscape itself.

Had Lambis designed it? She couldn't link the airy, welcoming spaces she'd seen, all capturing exquisite views, with the brooding, closed off man he'd become. Only the attention to detail, the insistence on quality in everything, gelled with the man she'd once believed she knew.

She lifted her head to the sun, shutting her eyes as she inhaled the scent of sea and wild herbs. The only time she'd been to Greece before had been on an official visit to Athens with her father. There'd been banquets and photo opportunities and the usual endless meet and greets. The closest she'd come to experiencing the magic of Greece had been attending an evening outdoor play performed in an ancient theatre in the shadow of the Acropolis.

But this place had a magic of its own. It was impossible to stop the bubble of hope and optimism welling inside.

Which gave her the confidence she needed to beard Lambis in his den. He'd been absent last night, excusing himself on the grounds of outstanding work. She'd seen Seb to bed early then dined alone in a charming outdoor alcove overlooking the sea and the pool.

She hadn't missed Lambis, not one scrap! But now she found herself reluctant to face him. Stupid to feel self-conscious because she'd told him what she thought of him yesterday, calling him on his selfishness and his obligations. He'd deserved every word.

Yet a lifetime of pouring oil on troubled waters, being gracious and diplomatic and always shutting her feelings away, had left their mark. That was why she felt…edgy at the idea of meeting him. It wasn't attraction.

It had been indignation she'd felt yesterday when he'd hauled her against him. Nothing more.

Yet through the long, restless night she'd found herself remembering the rich, intriguing scent of him as she'd stood with her nostrils buried in his shirt, her palms against the moulded, hot steel of that powerful torso.

Amelie swallowed and forced herself to face the truth. There'd been something about being held in his arms. A spike of…need, of desire.

Firmly she told herself it was an echo of the past. For though she'd once believed herself falling in love with him, they'd never embraced, never kissed. She'd once wanted that so badly; of course she was curious about how his touch would feel.

Now she knew. She could put it behind her, couldn't she?

She spun on her foot, ready to seek him out, only to find the man himself standing in the shadow of the broad roof, watching her. He looked imposing and implacable in faded jeans and a black short-sleeved shirt that revealed bronzed, powerful arms. His glossy dark hair was tousled as if he'd run his hands through it and immediately Amelie wondered how it would feel against her fingers. Soft and silky or thick and springy?

Her heart sped to a lopsided gallop and she clasped her hands before her as if to stop herself reaching out.

How long had he been there?

What was going on behind that impenetrable expression?

'Lambis,' she faltered, thrown by the little thrill of excitement that whispered through her as she said his name. 'I was just about to look for you.'

'The boy is all right?' Was that concern in his voice? Maybe he did care after all.

'He's fine. Still sleeping, in fact.'

Lambis nodded but said nothing. Not even a polite enquiry about how she'd slept. Which was as well as she'd found it hard to settle, even with the sound of the sea as a lullaby.

What had she expected? Smiles and casual conversation? There'd never been anything casual about Lambis. He'd always been intense, controlled. But once, surely, there'd been kindness and moments of tenderness. She remembered the rare sound of his laughter wrapping around her, captivating and enticing.

Amelie blinked and dragged her mind back to the present.

'I have a favour to ask.'

One dark eyebrow rose.

She repressed a huff of annoyance. 'Nothing too difficult. I need to get some clothes.'

A second eyebrow rose. 'There's no need to dress to impress.'

Amelie shook her head. 'I'm not interested in impressing anyone here.' She stared straight into those hooded eyes. 'We left in rather a hurry. I wasn't sure what to pack and—'

Lambis shoved his hands into the pockets of his jeans. The movement tugged at the dark cotton of his shirt as his shoulders and biceps bunched. 'Whatever you wear is fine. There are no fashion police here.'

She clung to her patience with an effort. Did he really think she cared so much about her appearance? True, she always took care to look neat and stylish in public, but surely he didn't think she was hung up on clothes? Hadn't he seen her yesterday in Anna's oversized jacket and boots, bundled up like a bag lady?

'What I'm trying to explain is that neither Seb nor I have swimsuits or broad-brimmed hats or anything for the beach. Seb loves swimming, or he used to. Spending time in the water might help him.' She tilted her jaw in challenge. 'We could, of course, swim in our underwear but it would be more comfortable and convenient if I could buy a few things. Unless you have spare beachwear?'

The house was beautifully furnished, with every small detail attended to, right down to fresh flowers and deliciously aromatic bath oils. It wouldn't surprise her if there was a room full of beach gear for guests.

'I'm not in the habit of keeping women's swimsuits.'

Which meant he was ruthless about ensuring his lovers' belongings were cleared out when each affair ended. Or perhaps they had no need for clothes while they were with him.

A little shimmy of…*something* raced through Amelie and heat spilled low in her abdomen.

Or maybe he just didn't invite women to his home. That was more likely. She couldn't believe a man as virile as Lambis, with that air of leashed power, would ever be short of female company. But it would always be on his terms.

'In that case, is there somewhere I can buy clothes? The town on the other side of the island, perhaps?'

He shook his head. 'Too small. You'd need to go to the mainland or one of the larger islands.' He paused and Amelie felt the weight of his assessing gaze. 'I suppose you'd like to fly out to shop?'

'No, thank you.' She repressed a shiver at the

idea of facing a crowd of tourists with cameras. Just one stray snap, one person who identified her as Princess Amelie, and the paparazzi would be searching the area for her and Seb. 'I don't want to risk being seen.'

He nodded. 'If you're after something simple and don't mind someone else buying for you, my housekeeper could put in an order. Our seafood is caught here on the island and most of the vegetables are grown locally but we get supplies by boat too. I can't guarantee the clothes would be up to your usual standard but—'

'That sounds perfect, thank you. It doesn't need to be haute couture. We just need something simple we can use at the beach. I'll go and talk to her about it now.'

Late that afternoon Lambis stood on the terrace watching the pair on the beach. The quiet little boy and the svelte, glorious naiad chatting as she built a sandcastle.

It was a quiet, charming scene, but there was nothing quiet or soothing about its impact. Apart from the fact Sébastien was as animated as a doll, there was Amelie.

Not haute couture, she'd said. Something simple. Yet she looked a million dollars in that swimsuit, like a sexy mermaid out to entice some poor, foolish mortal.

Reason told him she hadn't chosen the outfit

herself. He'd bet half his fortune it had been chosen by Costa, the guy who brought their supplies. It was definitely a man's choice. That bright lime bikini, outrageously brief and with side ties at the hip, made a man fantasise about tugging it undone and watching it fall.

Heat sparked in Lambis's belly and his groin tightened. He'd known Amelie for years, meeting her on his visits to Irini in St Galla. In that time he'd seen Amelie in ball gowns and designer dresses, in sedate suits and in mourning. He'd never seen her like this.

He leaned back against the wall of the villa, the effort of supporting himself too much.

All the world knew she was beautiful. He'd long ago realised she was too desirable for his peace of mind. She didn't wear revealing clothes but there'd been no mistaking her slim, womanly shape. Yet the sight of all that pale gold flesh, of those curves and hollows, of her breasts just on the verge of spilling from their confinement. And that waist, so narrow Lambis's hands itched at the thought he could probably span it.

He sucked oxygen into lungs so cramped it felt as if someone had tightened a lasso around them. His pulse thudded at his temple and his groin.

All day he'd locked himself away in the office, burying himself in work till his dormant conscience woke and urged him to spend time with his guests.

Not that he believed that would make a difference to Sébastien, but if it made Amelie feel better he'd do it.

Except nothing could make him go down there now. Not with an arousal the size of Mount Parnassus making every step painful. He might have managed to convince Amelie all those years ago that he wasn't interested in her, but the woman had eyes in her head. She'd take one look and *know* he wanted her.

Then where would they be?

She'd probably run a mile. Or if, miracle of miracles, she was willing to forgive his boorish behaviour, and the electric attraction he felt wasn't one-sided…

No. He couldn't even think it. A liaison with Amelie would be disastrous. He could never give her what she wanted. And he feared what being with her might do to his own carefully controlled and compartmentalised life.

He turned and walked slowly inside, the familiar bitter tang of regret on his tongue.

CHAPTER SIX

THE DAYS FELL into a routine. Every morning as dawn broke, like now, Lambis headed to the sea for a vigorous swim to clear the cobwebs of a night with too little sleep. By the time Amelie and Sébastien appeared he was always in his office. Evangelos Enterprises handled everything from close personal protection of VIPs to security for major events—international conferences to rock concerts and most things in between.

Business was booming, and demanding, yet it didn't hold his full attention.

Each day he'd emerge to lunch with his guests. It was his one gesture towards placating Amelie and her demand that he help her nephew.

Lambis knew there was nothing he could do for Sébastien, and it was confirmed daily when the boy avoided his gaze. There was no more tagging behind Lambis as he'd once done, leaving Lambis torn between relief and familiar guilt that he'd failed the child.

The rest of the day and evening was devoted to work and trying to avoid thinking about Amelie. With little success. The woman sneaked into his thoughts time and again, even though she'd given up demanding he do more for the boy.

Even now, as he powered through the clear waters of the bay, his head was filled with her, not his business. Not the trip he should be taking to LA soon, or the opportunities opening up in Asia, or any of the other issues demanding attention.

Lambis stopped, treading water, and flicked moisture from his hair. It was late, the sun already high as the silvery sheen of early morning gave way to the bright blue glare of another perfect day.

Amelie and Sébastien would be up and about soon.

On that thought he swam for the shore, cleaving easily through the crystal water. Nevertheless, he made a mental note to head to his gym for a long workout this afternoon. He'd spent too much time cooped up. No wonder he felt fractious. He'd always been a physical kind of guy, happiest when active, which was why following in his father's footsteps to become a bodyguard working for Irini's billionaire father had suited him down to the ground.

Hiding behind his desk wasn't his style.

Hiding. Had it come to that?

He hit the shallows and put his feet down, striding up onto the white sand beach. He drew in a breath, feeling the satisfied buzz he always got from exercise, the sun on his back and the scent of fresh salt air in his lungs.

He was actually smiling, till he saw the small figure curled up on the sand.

His heart knocked hard at his ribs and he faltered.

Sébastien sat with his knees up to his chin and his arms wrapped around his legs, right beside the towel Lambis had brought from the house.

The boy didn't meet his eyes but looked at a point just past him.

Only once recently had Sébastien met his gaze, when Lambis had a face full of snow. Then there'd been a tickle of…something behind the pale, blank face. His eyes had looked alive again. Now there was nothing.

That memory, and the urge to reach out and help the kid, ate at him. For once Lambis ignored the clamouring voice that urged him to turn and leave the boy where he was, alone but safe.

'Hello, Seb.' He cleared his throat and even so his voice came out rough. 'You're up early.'

Lambis picked up the towel and made himself stand beside the kid, rubbing his saturated hair.

'You're not going for a swim?' No response. He should be used to it but his heart clenched at the child's complete unresponsiveness. Did he even hear Lambis's words or was he lost completely in a world of grief and shock?

How hard it must be for Amelie to see her nephew like this. Every day, every hour, must take a toll, not just on her patience but on her strength and optimism. How did she keep going?

Lambis had no idea. He'd given up on optimism a long time ago.

He turned to survey the bay as he towelled his shoulders and torso. 'It's the best time of day for swimming. The water is a perfect temperature.'

Who was he kidding? Idle chatter had never been his style. He didn't have the skills to coax a traumatised child from his shell. As for Amelie's belief the kid had connected with him…once maybe. But there was no evidence of it now. Even if Lambis wanted to cultivate a relationship, which he didn't, he hadn't a clue how to go about it.

Once he'd had the knack. The glimmer of that memory was like the slice of a bright blade, slashing to the bone and deeper, right to his heart.

Lambis stood still, not even breathing, as he absorbed the familiar pain. It was long ago and whatever capacity he'd had for human connection, for tenderness, had been lost in the maelstrom of pain that had upended his life.

Losing both wife and child changed a man.

A distant buzz reached his ears and he frowned. Not a plane, and no one on the small island had a powerful speedboat. He turned, surveying the headland to the south. Sure enough, seconds later, a sleek powerboat erupted into the bay, still far enough out not to impinge on their privacy, but an unwelcome intrusion to the pristine morning.

Lambis raised his hand to shadow his eyes as he looked into the sun. The boat didn't veer towards the shore, nor did it slow. Chances were it was simply some holidaymaker from a distant island, out early with their expensive new toy. But he'd take no chances. He'd have it identified and tracked. Nothing, no one, would violate Amelie and Sébastien's privacy here.

He was already planning his first call when something, not a sound but a changed quality in the air, made him tense and turn.

It was Sébastien, no longer sitting curled up, but on his feet. His mouth had dropped open and his eyes stared as he tracked the speedboat. His skinny little body shook and his breathing was harsh.

Asthma attack? Allergic reaction?

Instantly, heart in mouth, Lambis was on his knees beside the boy, fighting back panic and dark memories. 'Sébastien? What is it?' Then, more slowly, forcing a tone of calm, 'Look at me, Seb. Can you catch your breath? Shake your head if you can't.'

In the split second while he waited for confirmation, Lambis was forming a plan. Carry the boy to the house, call the hospital, then onto the chopper and into the air.

Sébastien didn't look to him. His attention was on the boat. His open mouth worked. Not as if he were gasping for air, but almost as if he were speaking.

Lambis leaned closer, feeling for a fever but finding none. There was no sound except that grinding breath, an almost silent groan of air as if the very earth had ripped open. It made the hairs at Lambis's nape stand up.

Then, abruptly it hit him. The over-bright gleam in the little boy's staring eyes. The unspoken word his lips formed.

Mama.

He was remembering his parents. And another speedboat, not red but white and Royal St Gallan green, as befitted a boat belonging to the King.

That boat had sped across another bay, struck a submerged obstacle, veered dangerously and, before the proud new owner could correct its direction, hit rocks. The explosion that ripped the boat apart had been heard right through the capital of St Galla. Sébastien had stood with his aunt on the pier, watching.

Lambis gripped the child's shoulders as the boat disappeared around the next headland.

'It's all right, Seb. It's all right.'

The kid was stiff, every muscle straining, as the tremor grew to a terrible shudder. His breathing grew even more laboured, yet Lambis knew now it was emotional pain tearing at him, not some allergic reaction.

'You're thinking of your mother and father.' He dropped his voice to a low croon, the sort he'd once used for lullabies. A tone he'd have sworn he'd forgotten. 'It's not them, *agori mou*. Truly.' The child's distress engulfed him.

Did Sébastien even understand his parents were gone for ever?

Lambis saw the brimming green eyes, felt the raw, aching gasps racking the small body and gave up wondering about the right approach. Instead he acted on instinct, wrapping his arms around Sébastien's thin frame, lifting him off his feet and into his embrace as he sat down on the sun-warmed sand.

Tears came. Bright streams of grief, pouring silently down those too-pale cheeks.

Such soul-deep loss, such dazed heartbreak was something Lambis could relate to. This wasn't the time for words, but for the physical comfort of being held.

Briefly Lambis wondered if it would have made a difference, years ago, if there'd been anyone to hold him. Then the fleeting thought disintegrated as he put all his energies into comforting Irini's boy.

'It's okay,' he crooned, rocking that thin little body. 'It's okay.' When of course it patently wasn't. 'I'm here and Aunt Amelie is too. Everything's going to be okay.'

The child was fragile in his hold and something deep-seated in Lambis's chest seemed to loosen and tear. Lambis began whispering in Greek, for the words of solace and love came more easily in his mother tongue. And maybe Sébastien understood, for Irini had often spoken to him in Greek.

For the first time in years Lambis didn't guard his speech. He let dammed emotions break free. His only concern was this small scrap of humanity held close in his arms.

It seemed to work. That terrible tension in Sébastien's small frame eased, the shuddering, racking breaths eventually grew quieter, even if the stream of tears flowed ceaselessly.

Then the child did something that gutted him. He snuggled into Lambis's hold, hands curled up against his bony little chin as he turned his head into Lambis's chest.

For a second Lambis stilled, undone by the simple familiarity of the moment. Then, as ever, he shoved memory to the back of his mind and crooned again to the child who needed him.

Amelie stopped a few steps away. She'd been on her way from the house when she heard the boat and saw Seb's reaction. But long before she could reach him Lambis had rescued him.

Now, watching how the big man sheltered the tiny boy, those massive shoulders curved protectively around the child, buried emotions erupted.

She'd thought he hadn't cared, that Lambis was genuinely cold-hearted. How wrong she'd been. His voice, a continual stream of soft sound, was thick with emotion. She couldn't understand the words, but they spoke to the need deep within both Seb and her. The need for love and support. For comfort and sharing.

Lambis gave it all unstintingly, wrapped little Seb close, rocking him like a father would, ensuring he felt safe, even if he couldn't change the terrible tragedy that had orphaned her nephew.

Amelie's heart clenched, her mouth crumpled. Her whole being wobbled.

Even as gratitude welled for what he was doing, other emotions struck. *She* wanted to be held like that. She wanted someone to care for *her* as Lambis did now for Seb.

Not to tell her everything would be okay, for of course it could never be as it was. But to assure her that, just for a little while, she wasn't alone. That she had someone to share her burdens.

She blinked and made a conscious effort to cut loose that yearning. It was made immeasurably more difficult by the sight and sound of the man she'd once begun to love consoling her darling nephew.

In other circumstances—

No! She wasn't going there again.

She was made of stronger stuff.

She stepped forward, her shadow covering Lambis, and he tilted his head back. His eyes met hers, dark as a thunderstorm and cloudy with emotion. That emotion was a punch to her lungs. She'd never seen Lambis so…adrift.

Even as she thought it, he gathered himself. His gaze grew focused. He sat straighter, switching to English, and her fleeting sense of seeing the real man behind all that machismo faded.

'Look who's here, Sébastien. Your Aunt Lili. Didn't I tell you she'd be along soon?'

Seb's lack of response didn't faze him, but Amelie's blood ran cold as she saw her nephew's face. His skin was awash with tears, his eyes red and swollen.

'Seb. Darling.' She dropped to her knees, leaning in to cup his wet cheek, to smooth her unsteady hand across his bright gilt hair. 'Did the boat scare you?'

He let out a long, shuddering sigh, then, to Amelie's astonishment, nodded.

It was the smallest of movements but unmistakable. Her heart fluttered and long-dormant hope stirred. Her gaze lifted to Lambis's, so close, she realised, that his breath feathered her cheek. The heat of his big body encircled her as she leaned in to Seb.

Everything inside Amelie stilled, slowed. She became conscious of the minutest details. Of the long sooty lashes half lowered over Lambis's eyes, of the fine grain of his dark-toned skin and the shadow of stubble accentuating the hard angles of his jaw.

Sucking in a breath heady with male spice and the sea, she snapped her attention back to Seb. He was blinking, knuckling a hand to his eye, and love clenched her chest.

She'd do anything for her nephew. Whatever it took to secure his future. Even…

Not now. The future could wait. What mattered was making sure he was okay.

'Everything's going to be all right. You're safe here with me and Lambis.' She pinned on a smile. 'How about we go inside for breakfast?' She reached for him, but Lambis shook his head and she froze, abruptly aware that the backs of her hands touched his hot flesh where he encircled Seb. Belatedly she withdrew. Her skin prickled as if singed.

'I'll carry him. Okay, Seb?'

To Amelie's amazement, her nephew tilted his head again. It was what she'd hoped and prayed for. Some sign of life. Yet the reality of it was like a knife cutting too close to the fears she'd hidden since the accident.

It must be relief making her feel…odd. She sank back on her heels, blinking, overwhelmed, almost smothered by rising emotions.

'Amelie? Are you all right?' There it was again, that husky, beautiful cadence. Like a caress.

She cleared her throat. 'Of course.' It was stupid to feel overcome. She should be celebrating.

For too long she'd feared Seb might always live in that grey half world, separated from the rest of them. She'd been strong when he was stricken and silent. She needed to be strong now.

Her legs were stiff as she stood, and her smile felt as if it cracked her face. 'Let's all go inside and eat.' She didn't look at Lambis, confirming his agreement. After this he couldn't, surely, make his excuses and leave.

'That sounds like a fine idea. Swimming always gives me an appetite.' With an easy, athletic grace, Lambis rose to his feet, Seb safe in his arms, and turned towards the house.

Amelie followed, her gaze on his broad-shouldered frame. Every step revealed the clench and release of powerful muscles, of a raw, unvarnished masculinity that wasn't just about size and physical strength. It came from his absolute confidence and self-assurance.

Despite a lifetime's lessons in relying on no one but herself, in being the rock around which everyone else found safe anchor, Amelie found that incredibly attractive.

She paused and drew a deep breath.

No matter how strong, how appealing, Lambis wasn't for her. All that mattered was Seb and his happiness.

Amelie paused in the doorway of Lambis's study. Sunlight streamed in, lighting the vast desk, almost empty but for a computer screen and a phone. Clearly he was a man who preferred organisation to clutter. No doubt he managed his work demands with ruthless efficiency.

Her thoughts strayed to the decisive way he'd squashed her dreams years ago. He'd cut her off quickly, ending her tentative hopes and leaving no lingering doubts. Kinder, she supposed, than letting her wonder if he'd change his mind.

Amelie blinked and tore her gaze from the dark head of unruly hair that made her want to reach out and run her fingers through it.

He had his back to her, talking on the phone in Greek as he surveyed the view. Which gave her time to take in the rest of the room. It was simple, almost spare. Plain white walls and marble floor. Two jewel-toned icons glowed with an inner fire on the wall furthest from the wall of glass that looked over the bay. Beautiful as they were, the paintings didn't compare with the mother and child she'd seen in his mountain home. On another wall was a spectacular photograph of a sheer mountain top, with a tiny figure in bright climbing clothes, clinging to rock. Amelie felt dizzy just looking at it.

She stepped into the room and Lambis stilled. Moments later, his call ended, he swung round.

'I'm sorry to interrupt.' Her voice was too light, almost breathless, and she swallowed, determined to see this through. 'But I need to thank you for this morning.'

Lambis stood and instantly she felt at a disadvantage. Even from beyond the desk he towered over her. Worse was the difficulty she had stopping her gaze from straying over that powerful, muscular body she'd seen in all its glory a few hours before.

How many times had she berated herself for noticing? It was worse now, for she'd seen the tenderness he was capable of and it had evoked long-buried memories of the summer he'd spent in St Galla and the feelings she'd once harboured.

'There's no need for thanks. I did what anyone would have done.' His tone was brusque and his brow furrowed. Yesterday she wouldn't have looked beyond that. Now she wondered.

'Perhaps. But I'm grateful you were there. Seb was sound asleep, or so I thought, when I went to shower. I know you value your privacy, so I've made sure we wait till you've finished your swim to go outside.'

Lambis's frown became a scowl. 'You kept him indoors for that?'

Amelie shrugged. *He* was the one who'd made it clear he didn't want their company. He saw them only when they shared the brief midday meal. 'It seemed easiest.'

He raised his hand and forked it back through that shaggy mop of sable hair. No one else Amelie knew wore their hair like that. Her acquaintances prided themselves on their appearance, or made an effort to conform when meeting royalty. Lambis looked like he didn't give a damn how it looked or what anyone thought. Yet it suited him.

That and his still unshaven chin made him look like a marauder, a pirate. The sort of man who'd dare anything.

'Is that you?' She turned to the breathtaking photo of the climber.

'No. I'm not interested in photos of myself.' Something kindled in his gaze. 'I took the shot from the next peak up.'

So she'd been right. He *was* an adventurer. But not, she guessed, in business. There he was all about risk management, as she knew from the recommendations he'd made for royal security in St Galla.

'Was there anything else?'

Amelie stiffened. Had she really expected this morning would change things?

'I'd hoped to persuade you to share dinner with me so we could talk.' Amelie paused but there was no change in his expression. She hated the feeling she was a supplicant, seeking his favour.

'But that doesn't matter.' Might as well get this off her chest. Delaying would only make it more difficult. 'Mainly I wanted to apologise.' Amelie stood straight, meeting his gaze with all the outward calm a lifetime's practice could muster.

'You don't owe me an apology.' The scowl became positively thunderous. Yet, contrarily, all that did was emphasise the strong planes of his bold features. Even grumpy, Lambis fascinated her.

'I do.' She stepped forward then stopped. He

wouldn't appreciate her invading his space. He was putting out enough *keep away* vibes to power an electric fence. She hadn't missed the way his chin hitched at her approach or the curl of his hands.

Something thudded through her. Did he dislike her so very much? But Amelie was too proud to dwell on that.

'I accused you of not caring. I believed you hadn't loved Irini as she did you, and that Seb meant nothing.' His features were so still they could have been cast in bronze.

Amelie shook her head. 'For that I'm sorry. I was wrong.' She swallowed hard, her throat tight, and made herself continue. 'Your reasons for protecting your privacy are your own, but what I saw on the beach...that wasn't simply *what anyone would have done*. That was *love*.'

She hefted a breath and heard her words echo in the silence. It wasn't a welcoming silence. It vibrated with the tension emanating from the man before her.

'You care about Seb deeply and I apologise for questioning that.' Even if she had to bite her lip from asking what made Lambis try to keep the boy at a distance. 'You helped Seb when it mattered. Everything else is unimportant.'

She met his hard stare, wondering what was going on behind the dour expression. But what was the point? 'I also wanted to ask if Seb could spend a little more time with you.' Asking was difficult but Seb's wellbeing was more important than pride. 'This morning was a huge turning point for him and I don't want—'

'I understand. You're hoping to encourage more change in him.' Lambis saw it in her eyes, blazing with hope.

Her tentative smile tugged at him, made him uncomfortable.

'Don't read too much into what happened this morning.' Lambis felt his frown deepen. 'I'm no miracle cure.'

The idea was laughable. Deliberately his tone was harsh, covering the fact he didn't feel nearly as sure about things now as he had before. Where before there was certainty, now there was confusion.

These last few hours he'd felt emotions, yearnings he'd long ago emptied from his life. The feel of little Sébastien, clinging so needily in his arms. The look on Amelie's face, her gratitude when she'd found him cradling the boy, her touch as she'd burrowed into his embrace to comfort her nephew…

Tangled feelings enmeshed Lambis. Whichever direction he moved, whatever he did, they were waiting to tighten and knot around him. His breathing quickened.

'But you won't back away from him now?' There was real fear in her fine eyes.

Lambis felt the weight of her hope like a yoke across his shoulders. But how could he pull back now? This morning he'd simply been the one on the spot when Sébastien reacted. Yet he hesitated to say that. Stress had worn at Amelie, though she'd tried to conceal it. Pain circled his belly at the idea of her shouldering this burden alone.

He let go a long, slow breath and rolled his shoulders. 'I'll help if I can.' He forced the words through stiff lips.

His word was his bond and now there was no escape.

It was almost worth it to see the blaze of pleasure turn Amelie's face from beautiful to incandescent.

'Thank you, Lambis.' She opened her mouth as if to say more, then instead nodded and left the room.

Lambis watched her go, knowing he was doomed to disappoint her. That was his curse.

He'd inadvertently been responsible for his mother's death in childbirth.

Because of him, his wife and child had died before their time.

Just this year, he'd failed to keep Irini and her husband safe.

He wore guilt like a badge only he could see. Yet Amelie, sweet, caring, indomitable Amelie, believed him a protector, a saviour.

The worst of it was, he didn't have the heart to

disabuse her because all his battling had been in vain. Years of self-denial and distance hadn't succeeded in banishing his feelings for her, though he'd tried, for her sake.

He cared for her.

Wanted her.

Desired her.

He feared he didn't have the strength to hold back any longer.

CHAPTER SEVEN

AMELIE SMOOTHED THE fabric of her bronze-green dress with a hand that was a little clammy. She was *not* nervous to be sharing dinner with Lambis now Seb was asleep. It was just that the invitation was…unexpected.

As had been Lambis's arrival at the pool this afternoon. She and Seb had been in the shade of a huge awning, Amelie reading a story out loud and Seb curled against her. When Lambis appeared, striding out of the house in nothing but black swim shorts, her heart had thundered out of control and stayed that way as he sauntered across the flagstones.

His size and overt masculinity were almost daunting. His aura of barely contained power and raw edginess hinted at something wild and untamed beneath all that control.

Watching him stroll, half naked, towards them had been pure sensual delight. It wasn't just Amelie's pulse pounding hard in response. There'd been a throb deep in her womb, a quickening of arousal, and a softening as if her feminine core readied for his possession.

Heat flagged Amelie's cheeks even now, remembering. But Lambis hadn't noticed. His whole focus had been on Seb. Besides, she was a past master at hiding her response to him. He'd never have invited her to his home if he knew the number of nights he'd haunted her most erotic fantasies.

Yet what made Lambis Evangelos more devastating than mere sculpted beauty was the patient way he'd focused on Seb. He'd coaxed the little boy into the pool and, if Seb hadn't actually smiled or spoken, he'd responded, even at one point initiating a new phase of their game.

Amelie had sat back and watched, her heart full.

It had been easier when she detested Lambis for trying to turn them away. Now, as reluctant host, he was making a real difference to Seb, succeeding where she'd failed. All her defences against him, against further hurt, trembled on their foundations.

Pushing back her shoulders, she stepped out onto the wide terrace. This was just a meal. How many times had she sat through meals with complete strangers or people she didn't particularly like and made small talk? Yet a frisson of warning touched her nape as she followed the housekeeper's instructions to the far end of the terrace.

Subtle lighting turned the pool area to an idyllic retreat. But it was the scene at the end of the house that caught her breath.

A private patio extended from what she guessed were Lambis's rooms right to the white sand beach. A pergola draped with bright bougainvillea and other blooms gave the area a sense of intimacy and scented the evening air with flowers.

For a moment she hesitated, unnerved by the romantic scene, till she realised that, in addition to the fat white pillar candles in their glasses, there were lights everywhere. Clearly Lambis didn't want her misunderstanding and thinking this was some romantic rendezvous.

'Amelie.' A shadow moved at the far end of the terrace, prowling closer with that distinctive loose-limbed walk.

Her breath seized. In broad daylight Lambis Evangelos was stunning. In the soft glow of evening, dressed all in black and freshly shaved, Amelie couldn't drag her eyes away.

He stopped before her, his gaze skating over her dress and neat shoes, then back up to linger a second at her collarbone, where her pearl pendant rose with her rapid pulse, then up to meet her eyes.

His eyes looked darker than usual and for a moment they seemed to glow. She waited for him to say something, strangely disappointed when it was simply, 'Thank you for joining me.'

She inclined her head. 'My pleasure.' Stupidly she felt stiff and slightly breathless, as if her lifetime's experience in handling difficult social occasions had disintegrated.

Lambis, on the other hand, was a perfect host as he invited her to a seat at the table for two, offered wine and explained the aromatic seafood dishes prepared from today's catch on the other side of the island.

The problem was her. She was on edge, gauche as a girl on a first date. But this wasn't a date. This was Lambis being a good host. The change in him over a couple of days was remarkable. Today with Seb she'd again seen that quiet kindness that had drawn her years ago.

'Thank you, Lambis.' She met his eyes and held them despite the sizzle that fired in her veins. 'I know you don't want us here. I know you don't like your privacy invaded. But I *do* appreciate what you're doing for Seb.'

For a pulse beat, then another he was silent. '*Trying* to do. There are no guarantees.' The grooves at the corners of his mouth deepened. 'If anyone will make a difference it will be *you*. You're the one he loves. I'm almost a stranger.'

Amelie shook her head as she helped herself to the platter he held out. 'I haven't made a difference so far.' It took everything she had not to let her voice wobble. She'd failed Seb, and his dead parents.

'Don't underestimate what you've done.' Lambis's voice was gravel and silk, making tiny ripples of delight break out on her bare arms. 'You've always been there for him. He adores you. And I didn't trigger what happened today. It was the shock of the speedboat.'

'Perhaps. But he's responded to you. He's always responded to you.'

As she had. From the first moment Irini had introduced her to the imposing man whose rare, incredibly sexy smiles set her heart pounding.

'I'm a novelty.'

'More than that.' It was the essence of the man before her. A man she'd always believed honourable and strong, genuine when so many around her weren't. Hadn't she believed in him enough to uproot Seb and bring him all the way to Greece?

On the thought Amelie busied herself with her meal. Despite everything she'd told herself, despite him not wanting her, the wanting inside *her* hadn't died at all.

What a terrible time to realise she still had a weakness for the man!

'The fact is…' she squashed the feeling she was being disloyal '… Seb has needed a father figure for a long time. My brother Michel was a doting dad but there was a lot of pressure when he inherited the crown. He wasn't able to be with Seb a lot.' She paused and made herself taste some of the delicious fish before continuing.

'There's been a power struggle since my father's death between progressives wanting to update our constitution and the way St Galla runs, and more conservative elements.' Her mouth tightened as she thought of the current Prime Minister, Monsieur Barthe, who'd stymied Michel whenever he tried to introduce reforms.

'Irini mentioned something about it.'

Of course. Her sister-in-law had counted Lambis as one of her closest friends.

'Michel worked long hours and, because he was young, and people were used to my father's ways, not his, he had to work doubly hard at persuading parliament on key issues.' Her brother's impatience for change hadn't sat well with some of the country's powerbrokers. 'Seb didn't see as much of him, or Irini, as they wanted.'

'So you filled in for them.' He said it as if he already knew how it had been.

'Irini and Michel did the best they could. But it was natural they'd want some time alone together too. It was rare enough, given the demands on their time.'

'And the demands on yours?' Lambis's flinty tone made her look up, catching a spark of something she couldn't read in those deep-set eyes.

Amelie frowned. 'Only the usual.'

'That's not the way I remember it.' His eyes locked with hers and she couldn't look away. 'You were always there, ready with advice for the pair of them when they needed it, seeing to so many of the official royal functions, ready to lend a hand with Sébastien—'

Amelie's cutlery clattered onto her plate. 'Are you saying I interfered?' She'd done her best to step back from her previous role as royal hostess when her father died and Michel inherited. She'd *wanted* the younger couple to take their rightful places.

'No. I'm saying your own workload was enormous. You took on a lot of Irini's responsibilities as well as your own, plus advised your brother. I saw it for myself. Irini confessed she felt she wasn't pulling her weight.'

Poor Irini. Amelie's heart squeezed. 'It's not an easy thing to become royal. Besides, she was sick through her pregnancy. She did the best she could.'

'I know.' His face was set. 'I just wish she'd learned to say no to your brother more often.'

Pain lanced Amelie and she slid a palm over her ribs, trying to hold it in. He had to be thinking of the day they'd died. Irini had been reluctant to go in the new speedboat but had given in when Michel smiled. He could charm anyone with that smile.

'It was an accident.' She sat straighter in her seat and reached for her fork. 'Not Michel's fault.' Even the coroner had confirmed it. 'No one could have predicted it.'

Lambis surveyed her from under straight black eyebrows, his expression unreadable. 'As you say. An accident.'

Amelie reached for her glass and searched for an easier topic of conversation. Anything to banish those thoughts of 'if only' that taunted her when she thought of the accident.

'How did you come to build on this island? Is it where you grew up?'

For a moment longer Lambis seemed caught in the past. Then his mouth curled up in a hint of a smile and Amelie felt her insides flutter.

'Actually, it's here because of another accident. Irini's father grew up on this island, before he left to make his fortune.'

'Really? I had no idea. Irini didn't mention it.'

'She lived mostly on the mainland. But the old man built a villa right here on the bay, for holidays.'

'You bought it from him?'

Lambis shook his head then lifted his wine glass to his lips. Amelie watched his throat muscles work as he swallowed, fascinated that something so simple should feel so intimate.

'He gave it to me, along with a loan that allowed me to start my business. It's because of him I've got what I have today.'

'I don't understand. I thought you worked for him.'

'That's right. My father was his head of security and my mother was housekeeper in the Athens house. That's how I knew Irini. We grew up in the same house and were close, despite the age difference.'

Amelie took another forkful of her meal, nodding. 'But why did her father give you this place?'

Lambis turned his attention to his own meal.

'When I left school I worked for him as a bodyguard. I was here on the island one night when a fire broke out. There was a fault with the fire prevention system which meant the smoke alarms didn't sound and the sprinklers came on late. By the time I got Irini's father and the others out, the damage was irreparable.'

'You got them all out?'

Amelie watched him flex his hand, his gaze on a long scar running up to his wrist that she'd wondered about.

'It was simple enough once they woke. The danger was they'd succumb to the smoke.'

Amelie suspected his role hadn't been quite so simple, especially given that the scar looked like an old burn, but Lambis wasn't the sort to brag.

'Unfortunately the villa burned to the ground.'

'But Irini's father was so grateful he gave you the property?'

'He did. He didn't want to rebuild here, and chose an island closer to Athens for that. But he supported me when I wanted to start out on my own. For that I'm grateful.'

'So you grew up in Athens?' She'd expected to find him in the capital, not in the rugged mountains to the north.

'There and wherever his family moved. But for holidays my parents and I went to the mountains.' He looked up, snaring her gaze. 'They came from a village near the house you stayed in.'

'So you made that your permanent home?'

Emotion rippled across his face so swiftly Amelie couldn't read it, yet she was left feeling she'd missed something. Those eyes, almost warm before, now held emptiness.

'Lambis?'

He lifted his glass, taking his time to sip the fine white wine. 'I live there part-time. I have homes in a number of places.'

Amelie opened her mouth to probe then stopped. Having Lambis share so much of his past was more than she'd expected. The change in him, from the dismissive man she'd met in the mountains to tonight's host, was remarkable.

Was it because of his feelings for Seb? Or was there more to this change?

'Tell me about this proclamation ceremony. Can't someone else speak for Seb? Accept the crown on his behalf?'

No wonder Lambis was phenomenally successful. He always cut straight to the key issue.

'His Regent will do most of the talking but all the experts agree—' and she'd consulted them all '—that Seb has to speak too, proving he understands and accepts.' Was it foolish to believe it might be possible after all? The change in Seb today was dramatic, though he still wasn't talking.

'His Regent? That would be you?'

He *really* did have an uncanny knack for zeroing in on problems!

Amelie took another bite of her meal, chewing slowly before responding. Even now, Monsieur Barthe's position on this infuriated her. Hearing the Prime Minister voice his doubts had been a slap to the face.

'Ideally, yes.'

'But?' She saw his eyes narrow as if sensing her bottled-up anger. Surely she wasn't so easily read? But Lambis was an expert at that. It was an uncanny knack he'd used more than once to protect those in his care, according to Irini.

Amelie tore her gaze away to the straw-coloured wine in her glass.

'I'm the best person for the role and, I'd have thought, the only suitable one.'

'Of course you are. You're his aunt. You have a strong loving bond. Plus you were your father's right hand, and your brother's. You're the expert on what it takes to rule St Galla.'

Silently she nodded and eased back in her seat.

'That's a very enlightened view. Some people seem to think because I'm female I'm just…decorative, merely a hostess.' Despite the fact many of St Galla's recent reforms had been designed by her. Even when her father had been alive it had mainly been Amelie doing the hard work behind the scenes. Her father didn't have the patience.

'Whoever thinks that doesn't know you.'

Something in Lambis's voice yanked her head

up. He meant it. She read admiration in those steely eyes.

Amelie blinked, unprepared for the flood of delight that washed through her.

Oh, this isn't good. Not good at all.

She lifted her glass and took a small sip, buying time. Lambis's approval shouldn't matter and yet... She put the glass down, telling herself it was natural to be pleased she had someone on her side, though it made no material difference to the tussle for power back in St Galla.

'Thank you, Lambis.'

'It's the truth.' He paused and she sensed his sharp scrutiny, even though she busied herself with her meal. 'Are you going to tell me what's going on?'

Amelie's instinctive response was to gloss over her troubles. Life as a royal meant keeping them to herself, never looking to others for sympathy. While the St Gallan royal family was extremely popular, Amelie had no illusions. They led lives of privilege, despite the demands placed on them.

'Amelie?' His voice dropped, softening, and she felt something melt inside. Her caution?

What did it matter? There could be no harm in telling Lambis. He was the most circumspect person she knew.

'The Prime Minister, Monsieur Barthe, has made it clear he has concerns about a woman being Seb's Regent, especially a single woman.' She swallowed the knot of fury blocking her throat. 'He believes Seb's Regent should be a man or, failing that, he'd accept a princess of St Galla as Regent on condition she's married to a *suitable* man.'

Amelie's teeth clenched at the memory of his superior attitude and the misogynistic things he'd said, attempting to dictate her future and her nephew's. Then she looked up, startled, as she heard a stream of soft, rapid Greek.

'Sorry? What did you say?'

Lambis shook his head, his dark locks like glossy jet against his golden olive skin. 'Nothing for your ears, Princess.' His solid jaw was clamped as tight as hers felt. 'This man, Barthe, is a fool! He couldn't ask for anyone better for the role.'

Amelie felt the corners of her mouth tickle in a hint of a smile. It was nothing to the gush of heat through her taut body at Lambis's support.

'What's the guy's problem? Does he want to marry you himself?'

She couldn't help it. A choked laugh escaped. 'Hardly. He's sixty if he's a day.'

Lambis's straight eyebrows rose. 'And? It wouldn't be the first time an older man fell for a younger, beautiful woman.'

Amelie had been called beautiful, usually by a gushing press. It didn't mean anything, especially to someone whose father had been quick to point out defects in her demeanour, appearance or behaviour. Yes, she had even features and a healthy body but a lot of what passed for beauty was window dressing—jewellery, expensive clothes, makeup and a level of confidence.

Why did Lambis's casual reference to her as beautiful set the blood zinging in her veins? She even felt it scorch her cheeks!

'Our Prime Minister is already married, to a very quiet, respectable woman, who, I suspect, is a very obedient wife. Besides—' Amelie's mouth tightened '—he's already suggested he'd be willing to act as Seb's Regent.'

'The devil he did!' Lambis's scowl was ferocious but for once not in the least intimidating, since his anger was on her behalf, and Seb's.

Was she really so lonely that Lambis's support, and his good opinion, made such a difference?

'The man wants power for himself.'

'Absolutely. He's always been a schemer but lately he's interfered in things that don't concern him.' Like pestering her to marry King Alex of Bengaria, even beginning discussions with the Bengarians before consulting her.

That rankled. Amelie had signalled some time ago that she'd agree to *consider* an arranged royal marriage, *if* she and her prospective bridegroom were compatible. She wanted a family and her attempts so far to find true love had been disastrous. A dynastic match might be the answer. But, since her brother's death, the Prime Minister kept pushing her to commit. As if she'd give her word to marry a man she'd never met! What century did they think it was?

'What right has Barthe to dictate the next Regent?' Lambis's words broke into her thoughts. 'Surely he hasn't got the power to move you out of the equation?'

Amelie shrugged and sat back, giving up the pretence of eating. 'That's just it. I can't say for certain. I *can* say that he has a significant majority in parliament and a female Regent would be a first in St Galla. The country's views on the monarchy are still rather old-fashioned.'

'But your people love you! They always have.'

Amelie's mouth curled up at one corner. Strangely, it was reassuring to discover that Lambis, after all, wasn't infallible. She was so used to seeing him as supremely self-contained, competent and successful.

'Yes, I'm popular. But this isn't something the people will decide. There's a royal privy council, primarily politicians, who make the final decision. The majority older men, and a lot of them belong to Barthe's side of politics.'

'So you'll simply let him force your hand?'

'It won't be simple at all. I intend to fight for Seb's right to the throne, and my right to be Regent. The idea of him brought up by Monsieur Barthe or one of his cronies doesn't bear thinking about.'

Suddenly it was all too much. Not just grief for

her loss, and fear for Seb's wellbeing, but all the other pressures too.

'Thank you for the meal, Lambis. It was exquisite.' Carefully she folded her napkin and placed it on the table beside her plate. Then she moved her chair back. 'But I'm afraid I've lost my appetite.' Amelie gave him a small polite smile. 'If you'll excuse me, I think it's best if I go to my room now.'

She was on her feet and turning away when she heard the scratch of his chair on the paving.

'Wait, don't go.' A big hand closed around her upper arm.

For a millisecond Amelie's jagged nerves eased at the reassurance of that touch. Till she heard Lambis's hiss of indrawn breath and his hand dropped away.

Amelie stood, blinking at the view of garden lights and the dark bay beyond, telling herself it didn't matter. Truly. She'd had plenty of time to accept he didn't want her.

But that instant reaction told her more. It told her she actually *repelled* him.

What was wrong with her? Twice in her life she'd reached out to a man, believing they shared something special. Twice she'd been pushed away.

She blinked again, horrified by this curious stasis gripping her. She couldn't lift her feet. It was all she could do to repress the wild tumble of emotions churning inside.

'Why, Lambis? What is it about me?'

She hadn't intended the words. Heaven knew she'd worked for years to put on a bland, unconcerned face on the few occasions she and Lambis had met since that fateful summer. Pride dictated she say nothing, just accept she was flawed in some way that made her attractive from a distance, to the adoring crowds and the press, but not up close. Not to a man she cared about.

'What do you mean?'

Amelie counted to five, telling herself to forget this and walk away. She had enough to contend with without opening up this too. Yet how could she fix whatever was wrong with her, if she didn't know the problem? Was she doomed for ever to repel rather than attract?

On a spurt of defiant courage she spun on her heel. He stood close behind her. So close she had to hike up her chin to meet his unreadable gaze.

'Why don't you want to touch me? It's not that you're afraid I'll misinterpret and think you've changed your mind about...us.' She swallowed hard but kept going, determined to have this out. 'What is it about me that's so...' she waved a hand, searching for the word '...wrong?'

'Wrong?' His brow wrinkled. 'There's nothing wrong with you, Amelie.'

Yet she read strain in the tendons of his neck that stood proud. In the flare of his nostrils and the pulse racing at his temple. Amelie looked down and saw his hands bunched into fists.

'Isn't there?' She lifted her hand and lightly touched his cheek. Silky heat and just a touch of abrasiveness met the pads of her fingertips.

She'd wondered how it would feel to touch him.

But his instant step back told her everything she needed to know.

'Actually, don't bother answering.' She'd been wrong. She didn't need to know the answer. Tonight, with so many other insurmountable problems, she didn't have strength to wrestle with another.

She was turning when his arm shot out, barring her way. Again, he didn't touch her, yet it felt as if the air between them snapped and sizzled with electricity. How she deluded herself.

'You want to know why I don't touch you?' His voice sounded different, raw and hard. 'It's because I don't dare.'

Amelie frowned. 'What are you saying, Lambis? I don't understand.'

'No, you don't, do you?' His voice was husky. His hands closed around her shoulders, turning her to face him, pulling her so close she shivered as the heat of his big body encompassed her. 'I've tried to resist you, Amelie. I thought I'd succeeded, but I can't do it any more. Not when you're so close, so...' He shook his head. 'Every time I see you I want to touch you, *more* than touch you.'

Amelie's eyes widened. Her breath caught as he lowered his head. His eyes, the colour of a storm cloud shot with lightning, captured hers.

'There's absolutely nothing wrong with you, Amelie.' His breath feathered her cheeks. 'The problem is me. And the fact I want to do this.'

He hauled her up on her toes, wrapping powerful arms around her, then slanted his mouth over hers.

CHAPTER EIGHT

His mouth touched Amelie's, settled hard and demanding, his tongue probing till she—*ah!*

Lambis's thoughts fractured as Amelie's mouth opened under his, sweet and willing. Almost as if she'd been going crazy too, trying to stifle a longing so great it turned him inside out.

But that couldn't be. After his behaviour years before she'd washed her hands of him.

This was wrong, wrong, wrong.

He knew it. His conscience pounded out the word with every frantic beat of his pulse. They'd regret this.

Yet soaring delight undermined any hope of pulling away.

He gathered Amelie in, exulting in her soft femininity against him, the scent of her, heady as spring after eternal winter. The taste of her. Her gasp of surprise and pleasure. He leaned in, delving deeper, senses exploding at the nectar sweetness of her mouth fused with his, her tongue sliding against his, almost as eagerly as he devoured her.

Her hand rested on his chest, right where his heart pounded riotously. Then, in torturous slow motion, her other hand crept up his chest to slide beneath his collar, stoking his temperature to dangerous levels.

He'd known from the first that Amelie was a threat to his resolve This gentle caress of skin on skin proved it. He shuddered with the effort it took to stand there, merely kissing, when he wanted her touch all over him. Wanted to touch her all over and more, far more.

Her fingers slid higher, raking his scalp and the potent eroticism all but undid him.

His knees went weak and great racking shudders ripped through him, cracking what was left of his self-control.

'Amelie. Sweet Amelie.' He cupped the back of her head, holding it still as he bowed her back over his arm, lost in the give and take, the thrust and parry of their voracious kiss.

He could barely breathe, yet for the first time in memory his chest felt lighter, not banded tight by pain and regret.

She did this to him. This wondrous woman. She kissed like an angel and— No, not an angel, but a woman whose blood sang with need like his. Who'd pent up passion too long.

Lambis hauled her higher in his arms, felt her hand go to his shoulder for support as he lifted her off her feet and still it wasn't enough.

She was addictive. He'd always suspected it, from the moment he fell under the spell of her devastating smile and dazzling eyes, her lush body and charming personality with just the tiniest hint of diffidence when she spoke to him.

There was nothing diffident about her now.

Lambis backed her up against one of the columns supporting the arbour. Was that a hum of approval as he propped her up with his body? His massively aroused body. To his delight, she pressed closer, curving her pelvis against him. He shuddered, close to losing all willpower.

He'd dreamed of Amelie, spent hour upon hour torturing himself imagining how it would be to kiss her, touch her, possess her. Yet reality outstripped expectation. This woman was eager, responsive, as sensual as any fantasy lover. More. She was somehow more than he'd ever dared imagine.

The realisation was a blast of lightning to his frigid soul.

His kiss turned slow, inviting her to melt into him. All the while his head swam. She was sunlight and joy. Warmth and life after the dark well of nothing he'd inhabited so long.

Inhabited because that was his destiny, his penance.

The thought filtered slowly into his fogged brain and he almost groaned aloud as it registered. For how could he pull back when Amelie kissed him like this? When her fingers dug into him needily as he pressed his hips to her belly?

Because she deserves better.

That, finally, slashed through desire, through a wanting so great he didn't know how he managed to lift his head from hers.

The rush of oxygen into starved lungs hurt. So did the waft of warm air brushing his lips. He opened his eyes and his heart stilled.

Amelie's head rested back on a column, her throat arched at an abandoned angle, her lips plump and red from his kisses. A flush covered her face and throat and a tiny tic of a pulse shimmered at the base of her neck.

She was utterly glorious. A feast for the senses.

Lambis couldn't resist. He pressed his lips to the corner of her mouth. When she turned towards him offering her lips, she made his poor, crippled heart leap. The temptation to taste Paradise one more time was immense.

He had just enough sense to pull back and kiss his way across her jaw and down her neck, revelling in the little breathy sighs that set his groin hard.

The trouble was, at the base of her throat was more bare skin and from there the slope of her beautiful breasts.

Shaking with effort, not quite believing he'd finally found the strength to do it, Lambis stepped back, lowering Amelie till her feet touched the ground. His hands locked around her hips, securing her till he knew she could stand. Somehow his hands slid up to clasp her waist. He'd been right.

Despite her height and gorgeous curving femininity, Amelie was so slim he could almost span her waist with his big hands.

It was that reminder of her vulnerability, of the disparity between them, that finally forced him to end this.

She'd come to him seeking help not sex. She hadn't asked for this, no matter how unwittingly she'd tempted him these past days.

Days? Years it had been. Years of torture as he felt himself under her gentle spell yet knew they could never be together.

'Amelie.' It was a croak, barely intelligible.

Her eyelids fluttered. A tremor passed through her, then those brilliant jewel eyes met his and Lambis felt a heavy punch to the solar plexus. Not just need this time, but pain as he registered the question in her expression.

She swallowed then swiped her lips with her tongue. Did she taste him there? He knew he'd never eradicate the taste of her from his senses. It would torment him for years to come, when he was back in his own sterile world.

'Lambis.' Even the sound of her saying his name tested his resolution to let her go. Her hand moved against his scalp, a slow caress that sent tingles of sensual delight skittering across his flesh.

Amelie frowned, tilting her head to survey him from a different angle.

'Talk to me. Why…push me away then kiss me

like that?' Her voice was delightfully uneven, as if she were as thrown by this as he.

She deserved the truth. He'd always been honest with her, just not totally honest.

Some things had been better left unsaid.

'Why did you kiss me?' Her brow twitched and her mouth twisted. 'Because you're bored and I'm convenient?'

'No!' His hands tightened convulsively on her waist. 'You can't believe that. Convenience has nothing to do with it.'

These feelings were anything but convenient.

Amelie's eyes held his for what seemed an age. But she didn't move to break free and, selfish as he was, even knowing he shouldn't, Lambis revelled in the lithe heat of her narrow waist in his hands.

Nor did she remove her hands. One still splayed against his chest, the other clamped on his skull. Because, like him, she couldn't bear to break away? Now there was a bit of wishful thinking!

'You're attracted to me?' Her chin angled and Lambis realised how much her straight talking cost her.

'Attracted?' He shook his head, feeling his features settle into implacable lines. 'I've wanted you from the moment I saw you.'

He couldn't hide it any more.

Amelie flinched, shock widening her eyes. She would have drawn away except he wouldn't let her. *She was going nowhere.*

The aching hunger he'd tried to bury rose up, obliterating everything. His brain screamed he needed to release her, but his body acted on a primitive level that overrode conscious thought.

Instinct told him to forget conversation and claim the woman he'd craved for years. Take what, surely, her kiss implied she'd willingly give.

His hands twitched. To pull her close? To push her away? Lambis was on a knife-edge, battling for control.

'I find that hard to believe. You never said or even hinted—'

'I remember that first time we met.' His voice was a growl, hoarse as he recalled the effort it had taken to hold back all this time. 'I was with Irini when you walked in.' He'd been ready for a beautiful woman, but the reality had transfixed him. 'You wore a sleeveless white dress, belted at the waist.' That tiny waist he held now. 'There were green leaves all around the bottom of the skirt and little cut-outs between the leaves. You wore the same pearl pendant.'

The sun had caught her hair, turning it to gold, and she'd glowed with an inner radiance that had beckoned with a terrible, unstoppable power. She'd looked fresh as a spring morning and that smile of hers, the dancing delight in her eyes as she'd chatted so easily about the upcoming royal wedding, had cracked the icy carapace around his soul.

Even in those first moments, before he'd discovered she was as beautiful inside as out, Lambis had realised Amelie had the power to make him hunger and, worse, hope. That, above all, had convinced him she was best avoided.

Her eyes looked huge and when she spoke her voice was hushed. 'You remember that?'

'I do.' He remembered everything.

'I don't understand.' Her beautiful mouth trembled. She looked so lost, as if he'd suddenly proved the earth was flat and the sun circled the moon.

'It's simple,' he murmured. Devastatingly simple. 'I want you, Amelie. I always have.'

Lambis couldn't resist any more. Not when he read such hurt and confusion in her face. He leaned in and gently, so gently he shook with the effort of control, brushed his lips across hers.

Amelie's eyes fluttered closed as his mouth, soft and warm, touched hers. Instantly that tingling rush of heat filled her, that unstoppable longing.

She should pull back, demand answers.

But there was magic in his caress. In this butterfly-light kiss that made her want to lean closer and offer herself.

His hands tightened on her waist and shuddery delight surged. She'd never been held quite like this. Lambis's big hands around her made her feel small and feminine, sexy and…desirable. Amelie wasn't an innocent. She'd had a lover. But

Jules's youthful fumblings had never made her feel like *this*.

She slid her hand to the back of Lambis's head and pulled him to her, opening her lips and inviting him in. It was an invitation he accepted without hesitation, invading her mouth, and making her body come alive.

It was a miracle. Lambis and her. She'd wanted him so long. Liked and admired and desired him. Years of putting on a brave face hadn't cauterised her feelings. Even rejection hadn't ended those.

She was straining against him, rising on her toes, eager for more, when belatedly her brain began to work.

Lambis wasn't pulling her close but holding her off him, even as his languorous, impossibly sexy kiss invited her to lose herself completely. It was as if he seduced her, but at a careful distance.

This was the man who'd *rejected* her three years before.

Was she so under his thrall, all he had to do was crook his finger? There'd been no explanation, nothing but the bald statement that he'd always wanted her.

The fact he remembered the day they'd met, as she did, sliced through caution and sent her spinning straight into yearning. Amelie put her hands to his shoulders, trying not to savour their hard strength as she pushed against them, levering herself away.

His mouth lifted, leaving her breathless and shattered, gulping air. Her mouth throbbed and her peaked nipples strained against her bra, still seeking contact with his solid frame.

'Let me go.' Her voice was strangled, raspy, yet he heard. She felt him tense, his fingers digging against her ribs.

Then abruptly he stepped back, leaving her bereft and swaying. She still felt the imprint of his big hands at her waist and the rich taste of him on her tongue.

It had been tough, years ago, accepting his rejection with her head high. But this, standing so close, knowing he too felt this incredible pulse of attraction, tested her to the limit. His eyes shone with a silver light that promised passion and Amelie wanted it, so badly it shocked her.

She rubbed her hands up her arms.

'What's going on, Lambis?' He owed her an explanation.

His expression didn't alter. He looked down at her with the intensity of a mountain eagle surveying its prey. Did he see the way her flesh prickled on her bare arms? The way her nipples puckered hard and tight?

Amelie suspected Lambis saw that and much more. All those tiny signs of arousal she didn't even recognise, but he, a man with such a powerful sexual aura, must. Despite his air of self-control, of distance, there was no mistaking

Lambis Evangelos for anything other than a sexual being, a man of strong passions.

'Tell me!' Long repressed pain vied with recent anger. 'You say you've always wanted me, yet for years you've avoided being alone with me as if I was tainted—'

'No. Not that.'

Her chin hiked up. 'You rejected me. I didn't imagine that!' Oh, he'd been kind, or as kind as you could be when telling a woman you weren't interested. 'Either you lied then or you're lying now. I want to know which.'

He hefted a deep breath and rolled his head as if easing taut muscles. 'I didn't lie, though I was tempted. You have no idea how much I wanted to make love to you.'

Amelie folded her arms at her waist, holding in the trembling excitement his words evoked. 'You're right. I have no idea. You told me it was better if we didn't spend time together. That it would be a mistake to get close.'

She fought to keep the hurt from her voice. The memory of her tentative hopes and how he'd dashed them made her feel sick.

Lambis looked immovable, not lover-like, with his muscles bunched, his jaw set.

'You wanted a long-term relationship. You wanted someone to fall in love with. I couldn't be that man.'

Amelie's throat seized. By the time she'd confronted Lambis, she'd already been a fair way towards falling in love with him. Had he known?

'Let me get this right. You were attracted but—'

'I *am* attracted.' The timbre of his voice wove, deep and seductive, around her bones. 'That never changed. I've always wanted you, Amelie.' The searing intensity of his stare scored her flesh and made her heart hammer. 'But I can't give you what you want. I couldn't promise hearts and flowers and a lifetime together.'

'Hold on!' Amelie raised her palm, cutting off his words. 'I never asked for a lifetime together. I told you I was attracted and asked you to stay on in St Galla so we could get to know each other.' It had taken courage to reveal her feelings to the enigmatic man who was her sister-in-law's friend.

'You're saying you wanted a quick lay? A one-night stand?'

'No!' Why twist her words?

'Exactly.' He nodded as if she'd proved his point. 'You're not that sort of woman. You want a family, someone to build your life around.' Something flickered in his eyes as he uncrossed his arms and dropped them. 'You didn't talk about a permanent relationship but that's where you hoped it would lead.'

He was right. She *had* hoped.

As for a family—was that so wrong? At twenty-nine her body clock ticked louder. She'd long ago realised that what she craved most wasn't pomp and glitter, or even the love of her people, though she treasured that. It was to love and be loved for herself, as a wife and mother, not a royal princess.

'So you rejected me because…?'

'Because I'm not the man you want. I can't give you that and I won't lie and pretend I can.'

Amelie frowned, resenting that he'd withheld vital information from her, apparently for her own good, like some paternalistic…

'You can't know that. You haven't even tried.'

As Amelie watched there was a change in the man before her. She couldn't put her finger on it but it was as sure as a shadow blocking out sunlight. There was a flicker in his eyes and he stared down at her with none of the heat that just seconds before had made her blood sizzle. It was as if a light had gone out inside.

'I did. Once. It didn't work.' Lambis's voice rang hollow. It sounded so empty a shudder raced across her nape. 'I can't promise any woman love. It would have been criminal to let you believe I could.'

Questions tumbled in Amelie's head. But the stark, bereft look in those piercing eyes stopped her tongue.

Suddenly she remembered Irini talking about her childhood friend, saying he deserved his business success, not simply because of his drive to succeed, but because he needed something good in his life. When Amelie had queried her, she'd clammed up, saying only that Lambis had faced private problems but preferred not to talk about them. Irini being Irini, she hadn't betrayed his trust and gossiped.

Which left Amelie where?

'You don't want love? A family?'

'That's not for me. It can never be.'

This time, fleeting as it was, she recognised the emotion that slashed across his face like jagged lightning. Pain. No, anguish. Her chest cramped in sympathy. No matter the persona he presented, Lambis was a man who felt deeply rather than not enough.

She wanted to touch him, soothe him.

As if reading her sympathy, Lambis spoke again, his voice cool. 'I can't offer love or happy ever afters. He paused, making sure she had time to process his words.

'But there's something I *can* offer.' His eyes held hers and Amelie couldn't look away. 'Passion. An affair that would bring us both pleasure.'

'Sex without strings?' Amelie heard herself saying. 'It's not my style.'

She'd had but one lover, a man she'd once believed she'd spend her life with, until he'd betrayed her love and walked away, eventually marrying someone else.

Was that why Lambis's outrageous suggestion tempted? Because she'd never been lucky in love?

Or because she'd never got over Lambis?

'Why not?' His dark eyes held hers. 'We both feel this desire. We both…want.'

As he spoke Amelie felt heat flare low in her pelvis and a heavy, needy pulse begin deep inside.

'We wouldn't be hurting anyone. Why not find pleasure in each other's arms?'

His was the voice of temptation, Amelie decided as it rumbled through her, its echo eddying deep and low. She stifled a gasp at the way her body responded, softening, eager. Even after all that had gone before, Lambis had only to mention sex and she was excited, hungry.

Amelie blinked, fighting back emotions too mixed, too strong, to contain. 'I've heard enough. I'm going to bed.' Pivoting on her foot she turned away.

She was almost around the corner of the house when his voice feathered the night. 'Think about it, Amelie.'

CHAPTER NINE

Think about it?

She did nothing but think about it!

All through the long, sultry night Amelie couldn't wrest her mind from Lambis's proposition. Even this morning, busy with Seb, her thoughts kept straying to the idea of an affair. A hot, passionate, purely physical affair.

Her body said *Yes*. All but screamed it, as that betraying heat settled tight and low in her pelvis and a throb of anticipation started up at the apex of her thighs.

Yet her heart and her head warned of danger. From the first she'd felt drawn to Lambis, sexually and emotionally. Till she'd had to smother those feelings.

When, last night, he'd revealed he'd tried love and it hadn't worked, regret had pounded hard in her blood. Regret for his pain. Surely that was dangerous?

Yet the idea of an affair with Lambis was alluring.

Her thoughts circled as she tried to use logic and failed dismally. She *wanted* to take a risk on transitory, utterly selfish pleasure.

She'd spent her life being dependable, responsible and, in her youth, obedient. Her one act of rebellion had been when she was a university student. Even then she hadn't managed to escape the demands of duty or, more specifically, her father, by leaving St Galla to study. He'd insisted she stay close and act as his hostess so she'd studied locally, never quite accepted by the other students since, between lectures, she regularly appeared at official events in diamonds and jewels.

Only Jules had treated her like anyone else. Jules, the quiet medical student who'd wooed and won her. His lovemaking had been tender rather than ardent but she'd been so in love, so wrapped up in thoughts of their future together, she hadn't minded.

Not till her father stepped in, declaring it impossible a royal princess should marry a commoner. Amelie had defied her father, only to discover Jules had backed off, cowed by her father's bluster and, she realised later, a hefty payout to help him set up his medical practice. He'd dropped her unceremoniously, telling her he'd been wrong; clearly people from such different backgrounds couldn't make a marriage work.

So much for love.

Since then she'd guarded her heart. Until Lambis strode into the palace and she felt herself spin out of control, losing the battle not to fall for him.

The second time she'd put herself on the line, shoving aside pride. She hadn't waited in the hope *he* might declare an interest, but had made the first move. Only to be rejected.

Love clearly wasn't for her. The way Lambis had turned from her had been the final straw. After that she'd begun to think seriously on the Prime Minister's suggestion, more frequent in the last couple of years, that she accept an arranged marriage. It was why she'd consented to meet King Alex of Bengaria. Now, with the pressure to marry before being made Regent, an arranged marriage was more than ever desirable.

If she could stomach a loveless marriage. Surely it wouldn't be as difficult as her parents' marriage? King Alex was supposed to be a fine man, an honest man, not a philanderer.

'Is something wrong?' Lambis's voice interrupted her circling thoughts and she stiffened. Heat washed her cheeks.

'Nothing at all.' She didn't meet his look but turned to Seb, beside her on the back seat of the large rowing boat. 'Have you seen any fish yet, *mon lapin*?'

Seb shook his head, then, a second later, reached out and tugged her hand, pointing down into the miraculously clear blue-green depths.

Instantly Amelie forgot her problems, excitement rising. Seb was a changed boy since he'd cried in Lambis's arms. He didn't speak, but he was responsive as he hadn't been before.

'I see them. Aren't they quick? See how the sun catches them when they turn?'

The rhythmic lap of the oars ceased and Lambis leaned towards the side too. 'Well spotted, Sébastien. Do you like fishing?'

The small golden head turned as Seb looked up at the big man who took up most of the space in the boat.

'I don't think you've ever been fishing, have you, Seb?' While Amelie had tried to ensure her nephew lived a life as close to ordinary as possible, she'd never taken him fishing. She doubted his parents had.

The boy shook his head and Amelie felt again that tiny flare of hope. Maybe, after all, with patience he'd get through this. At least now he was interacting. It was a precious start.

'Well, if you'd like to try one day, just let me know. I know a secret spot the local fishermen say is the best.' Without waiting for an answer, Lambis picked up the oars and began pulling on them again, ploughing them easily through the water towards the headland.

It had been an inspired suggestion of his to take out the rowing boat instead of the sleek powerboat in the boathouse. He'd rowed it to the beach so Seb didn't have to see the other boat, so like the one that had scared him, and Seb had actually smiled at the novelty of wading out then being scooped up in Lambis's arms and settled on the back seat.

That smile had pierced Amelie's heart and she'd found herself unaccountably close to tears. Till she'd seen Lambis looking at her and turned away, climbing clumsily into the boat rather than accept his assistance.

The rowing boat had another thing to recommend it. She got to watch Lambis row. No matter how often she told herself not to stare, and kept busy chatting with Seb, her gaze slid back to the big man pulling at the oars. Every stroke emphasised the power in his arms and upper body, pulling his T-shirt across the fascinating play of muscles. His long legs stretched out so she found hers brushing them as she turned. And every time showers of sparks ignited under her skin.

An affair that would bring us both pleasure. Passion.

Excitement ripped through her as she remembered his words. Was he thinking about it too? Lambis had been particularly unreadable this morning. It drove her crazy, wondering if he regretted his words last night.

He didn't look like he'd paced the floor half the night, as she had. He looked rested, fit, and comfortable in his skin. Sure of himself.

Sure he couldn't offer love.

Again she circled back to that nugget of information, worrying at it like a tongue at a sore tooth. But what was the point? She'd long ago accepted he'd never love her.

'Here we are. Now, keep your hands inside the boat; the entrance is narrow.'

They approached a dark hole in the white cliff of the headland. Seb shifted closer and she put her arm around him.

'It's okay, *mon lapin*. Lambis has promised us a nice surprise. A surprise is worth a little adventure, don't you think?

Seb nodded against her side, staying close as Lambis guided the boat gently into the black entrance. The temperature dropped as they floated into the cave, and darkness engulfed them. Seb leaned closer.

'Are you watching?' Lambis's voice floated out of the gloom. 'Any minute now.' He paused. 'There! What do you think?'

Amelie felt her eyes widen as the boat turned a corner and suddenly the darkness retreated. Ahead was a bright blue bowl of water. So bright it seemed iridescent. Above, the roof of the cavern soared high till, where the top of the vast space must once have been, there was only clear Aegean sky.

'It's wonderful,' she breathed, her hand tightening on Seb. 'Spectacular.'

'I thought you'd enjoy it.' For a moment Lambis held her eyes and she felt her breath seize. Then he turned to her nephew. 'All this used to be underground, until one day, hundreds of years ago, part of the roof fell, letting in the light. Now it's a secret place, perfect for private picnics.'

Seb stirred, pulling back from her side and sliding along the seat to take in the magical view. Everything about it felt magical, from the crystal blue depths to the bright dome of sky above, and the sense of being cut off from the world.

The boat bumped gently against the shore and Lambis shipped the oars. Moments later he was ashore, tugging the boat in close and tying it to a rock. Then he lifted Seb out.

Amelie watched as her nephew immediately investigated the shoreline of a tiny beach beneath the overhang. He was on hands and knees, peering into the watery depths, just like any other curious child.

How long since she'd seen him like that?

'Thank you, Lambis,' she murmured as she stood and passed him the picnic basket his housekeeper had provided. She didn't try to hide her delight. 'This was a great idea. Seb loves it.'

A hand, large and callused, closed around hers instead of taking the basket's handle. Instantly longing tugged, hard and tight, from her nipples to her womb. One touch and the hours since he'd held her vanished. It was as if Lambis had kissed her mere moments ago. Her heart skidded against her ribcage and the feel of his breath sluicing down over her mouth made her lips tingle and part in unconscious invitation.

He focused on the movement and the lines

bracketing his mouth grew deeper. 'It's not just for Sébastien. Do *you* like it, Amelie?'

She loved it when his voice eddied down to that impossibly deep resonance that scoured her belly. Loved and hated it, because it made her feel on the edge of control. As if she were a creature of instinct, not thought. A woman liable to do something dangerous, like give herself to a man who didn't care for her.

But isn't that what you'd do if you went through with an arranged marriage? At least this way you'd enjoy passion with the only man who's made you feel desirable in years.

'Amelie?'

She nodded and slid her hand from beneath his. 'I've never seen anything like it. It's wonderful. Thank you for bringing us here.'

She waited till he turned to put the basket ashore then moved to alight, but he swung round quickly, catching her about the waist and lifting her out as easily as he had Seb.

Slowly he lowered her to the ground. So slowly she was aware of every plane and angle of his hard-packed body as she passed just a hairsbreadth from it.

It felt as if she'd brushed against him. All of her, from her hard nipples to her quivering thighs and clenched fingers, tingled.

Lambis's eyes held hers. He read her response, knew exactly what he was doing. It was there in the banked heat of his expression and the way those massive hands held her even after she was on her own feet.

'You can let me go.'

She didn't think he was going to respond. His body canted towards her. Then a splash broke the silence. Instantly alert, Amelie wheeled to look for Seb. But he was safe, merely throwing stones into the water, his tongue between his lips and his forehead bunched in concentration.

Amelie sagged in Lambis's hold, then the moment was gone. He released her and moved away, shaking out a blanket. She remained where she was, surveying the scene. The little boy playing his age-old game and the big man, apparently domesticated, setting up a picnic.

For a second, no longer, Amelie let herself remember the dreams she'd had for so long— children of her own, a man who loved her enough to mesh his life with hers. A man who was honest, faithful and caring, who saw her as something other than a princess, a diplomatic helpmeet or a trophy to be won in furthering his political ambitions.

She pursed her lips and shoved aside the yearning for what she'd never possess.

She had no idea if she'd accept an arranged marriage with the King of Bengaria. That could wait till she discovered if they were compatible.

Compatible was a far cry from love.

Who was she to cry for the moon and the stars? She had Seb to look after, to love. She had a responsibility to do what was best for him. That had to be her priority, not pining for the impossible.

Yet, as she smiled and joined him at the water's edge, she couldn't stifle a pang of regret.

Two hours later Amelie lay, head pillowed on her arm, watching Seb and Lambis in the water. Her lack of sleep caught up with her and she felt her eyelids droop. But she didn't want to sleep. Not when she could watch the pair of them, exploring the brilliant blue waters of the cave.

They were on the far side of the cavern now, two sleek, wet heads together, one dark as night and the other glowing old gold in the sunlight. Lambis's bare broad shoulders crested the water as he slowly swam breaststroke across the pool. Seb clung to his back, his small hands clasping dark olive skin.

Emotion crested at the sight of them together.

For all their differences, in size, age and temperament, there was something similar about them. The intensity of their expressions for one. The way Seb nodded in response to something Lambis pointed out.

And more. That almost impenetrable air of reserve.

Amelie frowned. In Seb that was a new characteristic. Before his parents' death he'd been lively and gregarious, a little chatterbox with an insatiable curiosity. In Lambis it seemed ingrained. Maybe it was the nature of his work, but she felt restraint and control, as much as a lack of demonstrativeness, had been part of Lambis for a long, long time.

Inevitably her thoughts worried at his words last night. He had tried love once and it hadn't worked.

Whom had he loved? Had the woman rejected him? Betrayed him?

It was none of her business yet she couldn't leave it alone.

Had Lambis always been so ferociously self-contained or had he once been lively and loving? Had he suffered hurt like her nephew and never recovered?

She remembered his rare, sweet smiles, usually directed at Irini but occasionally at her or Seb. They'd been like shafts of sunlight breaking through dissipating mist and they'd made her yearn.

It wasn't that he was bad-tempered, despite the awful, grumpy reception he'd given her at his mountain home. It was that he was…cut off. Completely self-contained.

The nurturing side of her wanted to break through to the man inside. The man who was doing more for her nephew than all the doctors and do-gooders they'd seen.

But Amelie had learned her lesson. It wasn't up to her to save Lambis, or heal him. He'd made it clear he was content with his life. He didn't want her help.

Just her body.

Heat slammed through her. Even thinking of it in those crude, unvarnished terms—two lonely people sharing sex—his proposition was devastatingly tempting.

She'd all but given up her dream of love, apart from her love for her nephew.

Why not take what Lambis suggested? As he said there was no harm—

'Look! Look!'

Amelie's head jerked up. Seconds later she was on her feet, heart throbbing high in her throat, straining to hear over the racing pulse that thundered in her ears. Eyes wide as saucers, she stared across the cavern to where Lambis trod water and Seb, on his back, sat up high, pointing towards the middle of the pool.

'Aunt Lili, look!'

Amelie swayed as if the very sea had risen to knock her off her feet. She stumbled forward, right to the water's edge, her gaze fixed on the little boy who stared with such rapt attention at the water.

Her hand was at her throat, as if to keep down the hammering heart that had risen there.

'See?' Familiar green eyes met hers from over Lambis's shoulder and it was like electricity jolting through her. 'See?' Seb demanded.

Reluctantly, not wanting to look away, Amelie turned. At first she saw nothing, then, from out of the shadows a dark blob emerged. She leaned forward, frowning. The blob swam closer and suddenly, despite her hammering pulse and the raw blast of shock reverberating through her, she smiled.

'I see! It's a turtle.'

Her gaze darted to Seb but he didn't answer. He was too busy following the animal's progress through the water. Did he realise he'd spoken? Her hand pressed down on her breastbone. She couldn't quite believe it.

'That's right,' Lambis said in a calm, deep voice, as if nothing momentous had happened. 'They come ashore on a nearby island to lay their eggs.'

Seb nodded, but didn't comment.

That didn't matter. He'd spoken! If he could do it once, surely, soon, he could do it again.

Overwhelmed, Amelie sank to the ground, her legs too weak to support her. Shock and relief confounded her and she blinked back tears. She should be happy, exultant even. Instead she felt horribly wobbly. Happy, but wobbly.

She'd spent so long hoping and praying for this day but in her heart of hearts she'd wondered if it would ever come. She scooted her hands up and down her chilled arms, feeling the gooseflesh there.

Her neck was stiff as she raised her head again

to peer towards the pair in the water. They were closer now, Lambis's dark eyes unreadable as he stared straight at her.

'Well done, Seb.' Her voice was croaky and uneven. 'You have very sharp eyes. I've never seen a turtle in the wild.'

'I think we ought to head back,' Lambis said. 'Your aunt is tired.'

'Oh, no. Please. Couldn't we stay a little longer?' It was Amelie who spoke, not Seb. She was loath to leave this magical place where miracles clearly happened. Seb was happy and relaxed here. Surely a little bit more of that magic could only help? 'Are you tired, Seb?'

He merely shook his head, his attention on the water, and Amelie told herself not to expect too much. Small steps were a vast improvement on none at all.

She met Lambis's eyes and found herself smiling.

Lambis stood in the shadows of the wide terrace, watching Amelie. The westering sun gilded her, turning her into an ethereal creature of gold.

She still wore the swimsuit and sarong from their trip to the cave and, as usual, it was all but impossible to drag his eyes away. Technically the filmy fabric covered her from where it was tied, just above her breasts, to just above her knees. Yet it teased and tantalised, giving glimpses of her toned body that meant he'd been forced to spend most of their earlier outing in the water rather than on dry land where his arousal would be obvious.

Deliberately he'd closeted himself in his office this afternoon, catching up on work. Allowing Amelie private time with her nephew. Now Sébastien was in bed and there was nothing to distract Lambis from this constant tug of desire.

Last night, after that kiss, he'd waited, hoping she'd change her mind and come to him. Accept his offer of an affair. For, God help him, it was all he could offer. That and this place as a refuge.

She needed, and deserved, far more. That was why he'd pulled back from her years ago, rather than pursue the intense attraction between them. But now, here they were, both alone, both hungry for each other.

Amelie had given herself away last night. She wanted him with a flagrant, earthy hunger that matched his.

He'd wondered if she'd be too refined to let herself go with a man, too fastidious for absolute passion.

Her response last night, her soft gasps of encouragement and pleasure, the demands of her beautiful body sliding against his, had been a revelation.

She walked the length of the white sand beach, then turned, looking towards the headland they'd visited earlier. Her shoulders hunched and her head dropped as she wrapped her arms around herself.

Even from here Lambis recognised her pain. It echoed through him too.

Damn it! He thought she'd be happy after hearing Sébastien speak. Had something else gone wrong? The thought sent fear crashing through him.

Before he could stop to consider, he was striding down the steps to the sand.

He might not be able to offer what she most wanted, but he couldn't leave her alone, hurting. Lambis's mouth turned down in a tight grimace.

Every day this woman taught him something new. He'd believed all the tenderness within him had died years ago with his wife, Delia, and little Dimitri. But here it was again, welling like an enormous tide, terrifying and unstoppable.

It had trickled over him as he'd watched Amelie at his mountain home, so brave in defence of her nephew, proud yet so vulnerable. It had flooded high when Sébastien had broken down, turning to him in his grief. Lambis had discovered anew the powerful, once familiar feelings of affection and protectiveness as he'd held the little boy tight. Then today, watching Amelie's face when Sébastien spoke—Lambis had been swamped by emotion.

'Amelie?' He halted behind her on the sand, so close he smelled the sweet floral perfume of her hair. 'What's happened? What's wrong?'

Her shoulders rose as if to shut him out.

'Nothing. Everything is good.' Yet her voice broke.

Lambis didn't wait for more lies. He stepped around her, then looked down into her face. Amelie's eyes shone huge and bright and her lush mouth tugged down at one corner as if she bit it.

'Tell me.' Distance was impossible.

She shook her head and golden strands of hair feathered her neck where her neat chignon collapsed. 'There's nothing wrong.' She blinked and forced a smile. He could tell it took effort. 'It's silly of me. I tucked Seb into bed and told him I loved him. And he...put his arms around my neck and told me he loved me too.' Her smile turned lopsided. 'That and those few words in the cave are the first time he's spoken since the accident. Isn't it ridiculous? I should be celebrating!'

'Not ridiculous at all. You've carried this burden too long.' She'd been so worried for Sébastien she probably hadn't had time to deal with her own grief.

Lambis paused. The old impulse to protect and care might be back but he was woefully out of practice. Besides, instinct, sharp as a blade to his bones, warned against getting involved. Yet it was too late. He *was* involved.

Sea-green eyes fixed on his and for a moment the impression of water and sky and the warm breeze died, as he lost himself there.

'Hold me for a little? Please?'

Without thought he moved closer, enfolding her in his embrace, pulling her head to his chest and letting his hand slide over the pure silk of her hair.

Lambis's breath faltered as she sank against him, her arms sliding around to hug him tight. He inhaled deeply, drawing in salt air and gardenia perfume, the sea and the rich scent of Amelie's skin. She nestled against him and he was torn between a trembling, poignant joy and the unstoppable, inevitable tension creeping through his body as arousal flared.

It was no good; despite his determination to squash it, desire rose. His body hardened, his erection pressing against her slim, soft form.

Yet Lambis stood unmoving, except for his fingers in her hair, gently circling and soothing, trying to offer the comfort she needed.

Finally, with a juddering sigh he felt all the way to his core, Amelie lifted her head. She arched her beautiful neck back and captured his gaze. Something deep within jolted and teetered, off balance. His breath stalled with the effort it took *not* to kiss her.

'Is your offer still open?'

'Offer?' It couldn't be what he thought. Life had taught him never to expect joy.

'For a no-strings affair.'

Silently Lambis stared down into her flushed, beautiful face.

Through the years he'd assuaged pain with brief sexual encounters, intense only in their carnality.

With Amelie any liaison would be *more*. Headier, more exciting, more satisfying. His arms tightened and his mouth curved in a hard feral smile of anticipation that ignored the warning voice inside.

Lambis knew happiness was transitory. Seven years ago God, life, fate had stolen everything from him and left him mired in an endless sea of pain and remorse. But not now. Not tonight, with Amelie bright and vital in his arms.

Tonight he wanted to *live*.

For one brief, glorious interlude he could have everything he hadn't permitted himself to dream about.

He didn't answer her question. Instead he swept her up in his arms and marched towards the villa, his stride lengthening to take the steps to the terrace three at a time.

CHAPTER TEN

SHE'D NEVER KNOWN a man like Lambis. The touch of those hard hands, his potent strength as he snatched her off the ground, beckoned to her at a primitive, visceral level. He held her high against his chest, the sturdy beat of his heart against her.

Amelie looked up at the beautiful, utterly male planes and angles of his face, and felt more feminine, more *cherished* than she ever had in her life.

Stupid when he was taking her inside for what she hoped would simply be hot sex that would obliterate her cares for an hour.

But it was true. Despite the fierce light in his eyes and the almost aggressive jut of his starkly defined jaw, she *did* feel cherished. And desired.

It had been ten long years since she'd had a lover. Ten years to lick her wounds and vow never to give herself to a man unless she was sure he loved her as she did him.

She cared for Lambis, cared too much. She was willing to throw over her hard-earned rules for a night in his arms.

She was fed up waiting for love.

Fed up being alone.

She'd take sex and the euphoria it brought. Even

if the reason she'd eventually agreed to his proposition was the caring side Lambis usually hid.

Amelie pressed her hand to his chest and his heartbeat quickened. She turned and buried her face against the soft fabric of his shirt and inhaled the intriguing scent of soap, earthy male and base notes of musk that set her trembling with desire.

'I want you,' she murmured. So much easier to say it when she wasn't meeting that piercing stare.

Movement rippled through him, like an earth tremor, and his pace quickened.

She smiled. He was as eager as she.

Then he shouldered open a door to the master suite. Amelie had an impression of white walls, a lofty ceiling and touches of turquoise furnishings before she landed with a soft gasp on a wide mattress.

Lambis stood above her, his shoulders rising and falling with each deep breath. His hooded eyes glittered.

'Take your clothes off.' His lips barely moved. If it weren't for the tension radiating off him, Amelie might have taken offence at his brusqueness.

Her eyes dropped to his hands, clenching and releasing at his sides, and the unmistakable bulge in his trousers. The bulge she'd felt press into her on the beach.

'Why don't you do it for me?' She spread her arms wide, as if casual sex was an everyday occurrence and her throat hadn't dried with excitement and nerves.

She refused to let her relative inexperience matter. Excitement skittered through her at the demands of this new Amelie, who focused, for the first time, on satisfying her own wants.

'Because,' he growled, his voice soft yet taut, 'I don't dare lay hands on you yet. I want to last long enough to give you pleasure.'

Heat seared Amelie's throat, climbing to her cheeks and washing down her breasts. Her nipples turned to hard nubs and she caught her breath as Lambis's eyes zeroed in on them. Her body came alive as if he'd touched her with that hard stare and delicious anticipation quivered the length of her spine.

'Then take off your clothes for me.' She couldn't believe she addressed him so coolly when she was burning up, her body melting in places she hadn't even been conscious of for years.

A muscle worked in his jaw and his nostrils flared, accentuating the proud line of his nose and the ripe fullness of those chiselled lips. Without a word, his hands lifted to his shirt front and yanked it open. Tiny buttons spattered her thigh, ripped off by his violence, and Amelie's pulse quickened.

Lambis shrugged off the torn garment, revealing that broad golden torso she'd spent the morning trying not to stare at.

Lambis was a big man. Tall, well-muscled, built

like an athlete. Not a fine-boned long distance runner but the sort of man who could wrestle or toss a javelin or swim. Broad at the shoulders, deep across the chest, his torso was a perfectly sculpted example of male power. Defined pectoral muscles, flat belly and tight abdominals. His flesh glowed golden olive and a light dusting of dark hair covered his chest then thinned to a narrow line that bisected his torso and disappeared into his jeans.

Her gaze dropped to his narrow hips and solid thighs. And that other solidity hidden by straining denim.

Amelie swallowed and found the movement difficult, as if her throat muscles forgot how to work.

He was magnificent, virile and outrageously sexy. And so different from Jules, who'd been young and boyishly skinny. For a second Amelie felt a flicker of trepidation, wondering if she was out of her depth.

Then Lambis tugged open his belt and reached for the zip of his jeans and Amelie was too excited to feel anxious. Slowly, deliberately, he undid his jeans, then peeled his clothes down.

Amelie's pulse hammered out of control and her breath came in little pants as he revealed himself. There was a tingling, melting heat between her legs and she shifted on the bed, pressing her thighs together as if that would ease the ache within.

Lambis saw the movement and his lips tilted at

one corner in what might have been a smile if his expression weren't so taut.

Finally he kicked off his clothes and stood before her, utterly, gloriously naked.

The symmetry of his beautiful body made Amelie wish she were an artist, to capture him for posterity. But as she took in those long, heavy thighs, the thatch of black hair above them, and the proud, massive erection pointing towards her, the urgency gripping her had nothing to do with art.

Her fingers fumbled at the tie of her sarong. The knot of it tightened, grew more uncooperative with each attempt, till her hands grew damp with frustration.

She jerked her gaze away from Lambis and focused on the fabric, finally tearing it open and tossing the material off the bed. As she did, he stepped close and her heart beat double-time in anticipation. But, instead of coming to her, he opened a bedside drawer and took out a foil packet.

Amelie averted her eyes. Not from prudishness, but from fear she'd explode from the sheer carnal excitement of watching him sheathe himself. She'd never been so turned on. Her whole body was alive with pinpricks of awareness. Even the brush of bed linen beneath her bikini-clad flesh was too much, and the rub of the material against her nipples…

'Take the bikini off.' His voice had bottomed out to that bass resonance that seeped into her bones and melted any last scrap of doubt.

Reaching back, Amelie tugged at the bikini strap, then, not allowing herself time to think, hauled the swimsuit top up and over her head, feeling the bounce of her freed breasts.

The hiss of his indrawn breath yanked her gaze around. His eyes were molten silver, hot enough to incinerate. His gaze travelled over her nakedness and she felt it as if he'd traced one big callused palm over soft flesh.

'Now the rest.' It wasn't a request but an order. Yet the harsh edge to his voice was a caress.

Amelie kept her eyes on his as she lifted her hips and wriggled free, dropping the scrap of fabric off the bed. He watched every movement with a hawklike intensity that might have made her nervous if she weren't so eager.

'Come here.' It wasn't her voice. It was the voice of a sultry stranger. Lambis lowered himself to the bed, kneeling astride her, his hands braced wide so his shoulders blocked the dying daylight.

Amelie shook, drawn so tight with arousal she could barely contain it. Just the waft of air across her bare flesh as he moved was like invisible fingers stroking. She smelt heat and musk and that heady, uniquely earthy tang that was Lambis.

She slipped her hands around his neck and felt him shudder. He closed his eyes, soft, incomprehensible words spilling from his lips. Yet she understood. This was both delight and torture.

'Amelie.' She'd never heard her name sound like

that. A groan and a prayer. Instead of being awed or nervous about their mismatch in experience and size, it made Amelie feel strong.

'Take me, Lambis. Now.' She shifted, lifting her hips towards him.

His eyes snapped open and it was like watching an electrical storm over the Mediterranean. Searing light and piercing brilliance.

Yet despite the glaze of carnal intent in those stunning eyes, and the pared back determination on his bold face, Lambis didn't settle between her legs. Instead he dipped his head between those incredible shoulders and slowly, deliberately licked her breast from bottom to top.

Amelie gasped, her hands tightening around his neck, tangling in his dark, soft curls.

He did it again, stopping this time to circle her nipple, making her bow up to meet his mouth. The heat between her legs intensified and she wriggled, spreading her thighs till they met his, solid on either side of her.

She tried to pull his head down, clamp him to her breast, but he wouldn't be pushed. Instead he moved lower, nuzzling her ribcage, pressing kisses in a line down to her navel where his tongue took possession in a caress that nearly undid her.

'Lambis!' Amelie had thought she'd known desire but, with each second of his slow caresses, she moved from eager to officially desperate.

Her fingers dug into his slick shoulders and her

hips lifted as he forayed further, licking her belly and planting tiny kisses across to her hip bone and back. One big hand feathered her inner thigh, sliding up to stroke her cleft and the wetness there.

Amelie shuddered, her eyelids fluttering shut as her breath snagged. He stroked again, sliding further this time, testing her, then his mouth—

'No! No, don't!' She snapped her eyes open to find him blinking up at her as if *he'd* been the one roused from sensual abandon instead of the one playing her body like a finely tuned instrument.

'You don't like it?' His brow furrowed and for the first time Amelie read something other than confidence and arousal in his features.

'Too much,' she panted. 'Please. I want *you*.' She had no doubt she'd have flown to the moon at the touch of his hand or mouth, or both, but that wasn't what she craved.

His jaw tightened and again she saw the fascinating little tic of pulse betraying his agitation. 'The way you make me feel, I won't last long enough to—'

'Good.' She shuddered. Just talking about it drew her to the brink. Or maybe it was the way his breath feathered her sensitive skin and his thumb circled the slick centre of her. 'I want you *now*.'

The words were barely out when he moved. Lambis nudged her knees wide then lifted her calves in his big hands, stroking then kissing them as he placed her heels on his shoulders. A moment later he rose on his knees, his hands gentle on her legs as they rose with him.

Amelie's breath sawed. His erection lay hard against her and she felt so *open* to him. He could see her stretched out before him and with her feet up in the air, her legs resting on his solid body, for a moment she felt scarily helpless.

'It's okay, *glyka mou*. I just want to see you.'

Lambis pressed forward and Amelie's eyes widened as the hot breadth of him stretched her, slowly, inexorably. Deliciously. Her breath stopped and something caught in her chest at his expression as he watched her. His brow puckered in concentration and his mouth twisted as if with pain. Yet still he pushed further.

Was it because Lambis was such a big man, or was it the angle at which he held her, that made his glacially slow possession so much *more*? Or perhaps it was the heat in his eyes, and his low moan of pleasure that made her heart palpitate and pleasure radiate in rippling waves.

He surged higher, further than she'd thought possible. Her fingers clutched the bedding at how impossibly good that felt. So good her inner muscles grasped him of their own accord and he stilled, sucking in a breath.

For long seconds neither moved, each absorbing the exquisite sensations of their coupling. Then, with a groan, Lambis withdrew.

Amelie reached out and tried to anchor herself,

grabbing his thighs, not wanting him to go. Her fingers dug into solid muscle as he retreated then, at the last moment, thrust hard and sure right to her core.

White light flickered on the edge of her vision. Her throat closed as she pushed high, impaling herself on him. Another retreat, another quick, decisive thrust and the flicker became sheet lightning, exploding around her.

Another thrust and another, his pace quickening, his possession so deep she felt melded to him. Amelie had never experienced anything like this. She relished every thrust, every caress, every second. His raw, urgent need and her own savage hunger to possess him. As if she'd waited all her life for this man and this moment.

When his hand dropped between her thighs, feathering that most sensitive spot, a spark detonated the long-banked fire within her. She called his name, needy and grateful, as he pushed her into ecstasy, into a place she'd never been before.

Seconds later he faltered, his fluid rhythm grew uncoordinated and he pulsed, out of control within her. Lambis leaned in, slipping her wobbly legs aside and took her mouth, tongue dancing with hers as their climaxes crashed through them and their bodies jerked and shuddered as one.

Dimly Amelie was aware of her hands lifting to tangle in his hair. Of the brush of chest hair and heavy pectorals against her breasts. Of the restless, almost worshipful stroke of his hand along her trembling body as she eased from ecstasy into a dreamy state of boneless satisfaction.

Lambis lifted his head then drew back but she wrapped her rubbery legs about him and hung on tight, refusing to let go. He didn't go far, just enough to kiss her breast. Instantly fire shot from her womb to her nipple and she arched helplessly against him, her eyes snapping open in astonishment.

Satisfaction flared in those silvery eyes, a tight, knowing smile curved his lips and again his hand slipped low. His thumb pressed her clitoris, circling, pleasing, and she heard her gasp of pleasure. Lambis leaned down, kissed her nipple then sucked hard at it just as his thumb pressed again and, to her astonishment, another explosion consumed her.

Amelie convulsed around him, heard her own high-pitched cry and felt herself disintegrate into wave upon wave of rapture.

Her only compass point was Lambis, his heat surrounding her, his breath feathering her flesh and his deep voice stroking through her. He whispered words she couldn't translate but knew instinctively were endearments.

Strong arms surrounded her, pulling her to him as he rolled over and clamped her to his chest. Amelie never wanted to move again.

How long she lay in that blissful state, Amelie

didn't know. She might even have slept. Finally she became aware of change, of movement. She was in Lambis's arms, her face turned instinctively into that solid wall of hot, honed muscle that was his chest. The steady rhythm of his heart reassured, as did the way he held her, sure and safe as he crossed the room.

Amelie smiled muzzily, still overcome by the glow of wellbeing that had been his gift to her.

Then to her amazement she felt water against her heels. Her eyes shot open. They were in a vast bathroom, softly lit by candles. Lambis had run her a bath while she slept.

'I didn't think you were a candle person.' Her words were slurred. Yet even as she said it she remembered how they'd dined by candlelight.

Lambis huffed and she heard a smile in his voice. 'My housekeeper is. But it seemed right to use them tonight.'

With that he lowered her into the deep, warm bath.

Amelie didn't try to stop the sigh of pleasure as she sank below the surface. Before she could settle, Lambis stepped in behind her, pulling her back against him so she reclined between his long legs, one of his arms wrapped around her waist.

She let her head loll back against his shoulder, concentrating only on this moment, coveting this interlude of peace and…oneness.

No, she wouldn't think about that, how from the moment on the beach she'd felt...connected.

'This is perfect,' she purred. 'How did you know?' She'd been incapable of coherent thought after their urgent, explosive coupling.

She felt him shrug. When he spoke, the sound rumbled up inside him, making her smile. 'I wondered if you might be sore. I'm not a small man and you were...tight.' His voice dropped to that bass note she loved. It sent desire quaking through her.

'Amelie?' Definitely concern in his voice. '*Are you okay?*'

'Yes.' Now he mentioned it, she was achy between the thighs and her muscles felt well-used, as if she'd spent a long session in the gym. But that was nothing to the hum of delight in her pleasure-hazed body. 'Lovely.'

'Truly? I should have been gentler.'

Amelie roused and she slid her arm over his where it circled her waist. 'You didn't hurt me. And I was too hungry for you to care about gentle.' A tiny smile caught her lips. 'My only other experience was so gentle it was almost a non-event.'

Hazily she realised she was letting slip information she'd never shared with anyone. Never even voiced to herself. But in this candlelit room, seduced by the luxury of Lambis's closeness and the sensual heat of the water, that didn't seem important.

'You've only had sex once before?' He stiffened, his voice shocked.

Amelie patted his hand and ran her other hand down the muscled thigh beside her, intrigued by its shape and the way it twitched beneath her hand.

'No. More than once. But with the same man. Jules. And it was a long time ago.' She frowned, calculating. 'Ten years.'

Lambis said nothing, yet she heard him thinking. His heart rate quickened and the arm holding her curved closer.

'You were celibate for ten years and you suddenly give yourself to *me*?'

Now she heard it, an echo of something that might even have been fear, if she didn't know Lambis was scared of nothing.

'Don't read too much into it, Lambis. I'm not expecting hearts and flowers. I know this is a no-strings arrangement.' Even so, looking around the candlelit room, inhaling the seductive scent of the bath salts he'd thought to use for her, Amelie knew Lambis wasn't as unfeeling as he pretended. He'd taken time to think about how she felt and what would please her.

'I don't regret what we've done.' Far from it. Making love with Lambis—no, having sex—was an experience she wouldn't have missed for anything.

'Who was this Jules?' His voice was gruff.

She shrugged, aware of the way her shoulder

blades slid up over his chest and his hand relaxed a little to splay over her stomach. A tiny trickle of awareness stirred within and she shifted in his hold.

Seconds passed. Why not tell him? Lambis was one of the few people she'd trust not to reveal secrets. She'd never had the luxury of a confidante. Irini, lovely as she was, had continually looked to her for support and guidance. Amelie hadn't felt able to unburden her own troubles.

'Jules was a medical student when I was at university in St Galla.'

'He swept you off your feet?' Lambis's breath feathered her scalp. Strange how that tiny sensation made her flesh prickle.

'Not exactly. Jules wasn't one for dramatic gestures. But he was kind and funny and he didn't treat me like a princess.' That didn't come out right. 'I mean, he didn't care about my title or connections. He saw *me*, liked me for who I was.' How appealing that had been. To her father she'd been an asset to be trotted out for official occasions, playing royal hostess after her mother's death and, as time passed, doing more and more of the behind the scenes work he couldn't be bothered with.

'We were engaged.' Amelie blinked, surprised the words slipped out.

'Yet you didn't marry?' Lambis's deep voice wrapped around her like his embrace.

Funny how easy it was to share confidences with him.

'No.' She strove to keep emotion from her voice. 'My father didn't approve. He was of the old school, insisting a princess of St Galla marry another royal, not a commoner. He persuaded Jules to leave.'

Silence. Finally Lambis spoke. 'You felt betrayed. That's why you haven't been with another man?'

Amelie's mouth twisted. 'I couldn't blame Jules. He was a poor student. Who could expect him to stand up against a king?' Yet that didn't stop the flutter of remembered distress, the echo of shattered dreams and the sense of betrayal. She'd stood up to the King. She'd been prepared to walk away from the palace, her title, any financial support, since that was what her father had threatened. She'd have left with only the clothes on her back if she had to, because she'd believed in Jules, believed in *them*.

She drew a shuddery breath and shook her head. 'I was naïve. I thought he loved me and we'd be together no matter what. Instead he said he'd made a mistake. He'd come into a sudden…inheritance and was moving to the far end of St Galla to set up as a GP.' She injected a lighter note into her voice. 'Last I heard he was married, with a brood of children.'

Lambis said nothing, merely lifted her hair from

her shoulder and pressed his lips there. Instantly a fine wire of tension pulled taut from the spot straight down to her pelvis. Her head angled back against him.

'He soured you off men.'

Again Amelie shrugged. It was true, but she hated him imagining her as some tragedy queen. 'You'd be surprised how few opportunities I have to be intimate. Everywhere I go the press are watching. Every holiday is just a couple of days tacked on to the end of official engagements. It's hard to get to know men away from my royal responsibilities and I've never been interested in a purely sexual affair, or one conducted under the press spotlight.'

The exception had been Lambis. But he'd shied from her and her desire for a meaningful relationship.

He wasn't shying now. She lowered her hand to his other leg, stroking and delighting in the shifting bunch of his muscles that told her he wasn't immune to her touch. Behind her his erection stirred. Her inner muscles clenched.

'Why now?' He breathed against her shoulder, his breath humid and seductive on her shivery flesh. 'Why me?'

Why Lambis? Because, despite what she'd told herself, it had always been Lambis, from the moment he'd walked into her life. She'd tried to obliterate her feelings but hadn't succeeded. All she could do was accept she still had a weakness for him and hope their affair would cure her of it.

'Because I've given up on love.' Saying the words made her feel strong, despite the pang of distress. 'It's not for me.' If she made it her mantra one day she'd convince herself.

'But you want a husband and children, surely? A family? I see it in you when you're with Sébastien.'

Damn the man for being so perceptive. And for forcing this issue. *He* was the one, with Jules, who'd trampled her romantic dreams. What did he want? Reassurance she wasn't hoping he'd change his mind and offer her more than sex?

Amelie moved to sit straighter and put distance between them but Lambis tightened his arm around her middle and for some reason she let him pull her back.

Face it, you like being held by him! Even when you feel you shouldn't.

'Well, I've got Seb to look after, haven't I? And if I want more I can go the old-fashioned route. Our Prime Minister has already suggested an arranged marriage with another royal.'

'You? In an arranged marriage?' Again that note of shock. For some reason it pleased Amelie that she'd surprised Lambis. She hated the idea of being an open book to a man who kept so much of himself hidden.

'Why not?'

His answer, when it came, stunned her. 'Because

you need love. You're the sort of woman who devotes her life to those she cares about. You deserve someone who'll care for you too. Someone who will fight for you, no matter what the odds.' There was a resonance about his words that spoke of deep feeling, and conviction, and it melted the frost of indignation forming around her heart.

See? He really is a nice guy.

He does care, even if only from a distance.

He wants you to be happy, even if he can't be the man you want.

Yet it would be a terrible mistake to read more into his concern. She might still yearn but he couldn't give her what she needed. Pain squeezed her chest.

She had to live for the moment. Enjoy this liaison to the full then walk away with her head high.

Deliberately she stroked her fingers up his thighs, trailing higher and higher till he shifted.

'You'd better not do that,' he growled. 'It's difficult enough already just holding you and not doing any more.'

'You mean sex?'

His erection twitched, making Amelie smile.

'I'm trying to restrain myself.' It sounded as if he spoke through gritted teeth and Amelie's smile widened. She loved that he made her feel desirable.

'What if I don't want you restrained?'

CHAPTER ELEVEN

LAMBIS CLENCHED HIS jaw and prayed for control.

Amelie's words threatened to undo him.

All through this conversation he'd struggled against baser instincts that urged him to take her again, *now*, but he'd held back.

The shock in her eyes when he'd positioned her on the bed, the exquisite tightness of her inner muscles, had proved what she'd since revealed, that she was a sexual novice.

'I don't want to hurt you, Amelie.' The words ground from him. That was why he'd tried to keep his distance, right from the start. Yet there was an inevitability about them together that he couldn't deny. There'd always been something about her, a brightness and gentle tenderness, that attracted him.

He hadn't been gentle. He felt guilty about that, but not enough. For she'd surprised him with her eagerness.

'You won't hurt me. I know you won't. Besides, we don't have much time. Seb and I must return to St Galla soon. We can't stay away indefinitely.'

Strange that, instead of satisfaction, her words unsettled him.

'I want to have sex with you again.' Did she

know how those words struck home? His already hard groin hardened even further. It was all he could do not to grind himself against her. 'I want to learn more.'

'Learn?' Lambis was so busy trying to control himself.

'Yes.' One of those delicate hands crept round behind her and circled his shaft. Lambis shut his eyes and shuddered. This felt impossibly good. 'Before tonight my sexual experience was very limited.'

The idea of being Amelie's sexual tutor should have delighted him. It did. Except Lambis felt far too close to the edge. Amelie was dainty and inexperienced and he was—

Her fingers tightened, sliding up in a long voluptuous stroke that had him groaning aloud.

On the other hand, she'd welcomed his carnality, with an ardour that stunned and excited. Far from being the fragile creature he'd once imagined, Amelie surprised him again and again with her strength, facing him down, calling him on his behaviour instead of shrinking back.

She stroked him again and he was lost. 'Turn around,' he ordered through gritted teeth, hands rising to her waist, turning her. Water splashed over the side of the bath and limbs tangled.

Then she was kneeling above him, slick and wet, her tip-tilted breasts glowing pink and glossy from the warm water. He traced a line from her breastbone down to her navel, then over her smooth belly to the triangle of dark golden hair just visible above the water.

Amelie shuddered as he stroked her there, her eyes growing heavy-lidded, her hips circling.

Did she have any idea how beautiful she looked, with her long golden hair falling damp around her breasts and her eyes foggy with arousal?

She leaned over, putting her hands on his shoulders and made to lower herself, but he stopped her. Watching her in the bedroom, writhing with the climaxes he'd given her, made him hungry for more.

Holding her hips, he moved forward, exploring that secret cleft with his tongue. She jolted as if an electric current passed through her and his erection throbbed in response. Again he licked, this time parting her folds and finding that tiny, sensitive pearl. Her heat enveloped him, her scent, the tremors of her body as he licked again, harder this time, and her fingers clawed at his shoulders.

'Lambis!' It was a gasp and a cry of tension as that judder came again and she tilted towards him. This time he kissed her, open-mouthed, drawing at her core until the soft cries became a scream and he heard his name echo again and again around the room.

Amelie shook against him, her breath tiny sobs that took his creaky heart and wrung it.

Tenderly, carefully, he drew her down into the

warm water and kissed her, absorbing those final shudders of ecstasy, his heart sprinting. Then he rose, reached across and grabbed the condom he'd left near the bath.

When he was sheathed he sat, moving down till her knees were either side of his hips and he nudged against her. One gentle tug and she slid down, enveloping him, drawing him home. He felt heat and wonder and a sense of rightness that was new, yet familiar.

That was when he saw the glitter of tears staining her cheeks and he wrapped his arms around her, his chest turning over.

'Don't cry, *glyka mou*. It's okay. I'll make it okay.'

He hadn't hurt her. He was sure he hadn't. Yet he stilled.

Amelie's eyes opened and he stared into brilliant, overfull pools of green. Her dark lashes were spiked and wet. But she managed a tremulous smile and feathered one shaky hand across his lips in a caress that tugged at long-hoarded emotions in his locked heart.

'It's more than okay, Lambis. I didn't know anything could feel like this.' Her mouth twisted. 'I know it's only sex,' she whispered, 'but you make me feel...' She shook her head, her lips firming, leaving him wondering just how he made her feel.

He didn't wonder long for she leaned in and kissed him, slowly, thoroughly, gratefully, and he felt the most uncommon sensations rise and whirl about him.

Then she was rocking against him, partly drawn by his insistent hands, but following a rhythm all her own. Lambis bucked up in time with each swing of her hips, rejoicing in the little circling movement she made that prolonged the ecstasy of their joining.

Still she kissed him, her hands cupping his face, her mouth sharing choked little mews of feminine satisfaction that had to be the sweetest, most erotic sound.

Lambis urged her faster, and she complied with that little shimmy of her hips that drove him harder and wilder against her. Till finally he could take no more, despite his determination to please her first. His climax erupted monumentally, throbbing so hard his head whirled at the euphoria of losing himself inside Amelie. He grabbed the back of her head, kissing her with such passion he shook with it. Then he felt the clutch of her orgasm around him and the bliss of it undid him.

Lambis lay on his back watching the first greypink light of dawn creep across the room. Amelie lay in his arms, her thick blonde hair draped like silk over his chest and shoulders, her body sprawled across him.

Through the evening and the night that followed they'd been insatiable. One touch, one soft sigh had been all it took for his libido to fire and, to his delight, Amelie had been just as eager.

Was it because neither had had a recent lover?

He found her long celibacy incredible. Despite her demure façade, Amelie was highly sexed, a woman who gave her all to a lover.

She wasn't the woman he'd imagined her. His first impression, apart from instant interest and just as instant lust, was that Amelie was charming but reserved, caring of her family and dutiful. He remembered her sweet diffidence as she'd suggested he stay on in St Galla so they could explore the attraction between them.

Somehow he'd never recognised the fire in her. The Amelie he'd begun to know in Greece was more like a firecracker, gunpowder hidden inside a decorative casing. Her temper, the way she'd refused to take no for an answer about getting him to help her nephew, had surprised. He was used to seeing her easy smile and diplomacy as she helped her brother manage his kingdom. Her love for her family had cemented the idea of her as a nurturer.

Her sexual passion had been a revelation, as had her stark honesty. His mind still reeled with some of the things she'd revealed.

Lambis's mouth tightened when he recalled her tears as they'd made love. It was easy to ascribe them to an excess of passion, to the shock of ecstasy after long celibacy. But it was more. Despite her feisty determination, Amelie was vulnerable. She grieved for her brother and on top of that worried over Sébastien.

Lambis's conscience warned he should back off. He was taking advantage of her when she was needy.

Yet, despite the grate of his conscience, he couldn't pull back. For so long he'd lived in his bleak, lonely world. It was where he deserved to be, of course. But now Amelie had smashed down the wall cutting him off from the world, it was beyond him to rebuild it.

Soon. He'd do it soon. A principled man would pull away from her, knowing she was better off without him. But Lambis had long ago faced the truth that he was brutally flawed. It wasn't right, but he'd take what he could from her, live this bright brief moment of pleasure.

He tugged the sheet up her bare back, lingering at the sweet indentation of her waist. So slender and supple yet strong. Amelie had been a miracle in his arms, reminding him how poignantly beautiful life could be.

He'd forgotten that in the years since he'd lost Delia and Dimitri. Pain and guilt had cast a pall over even his most precious memories. But, spending time with Amelie and Sébastien, Lambis had begun to remember the joy that had once been so intrinsic in his world. How caring and being cared for could transform you.

Lambis looked down at Amelie's head, nestled trustingly on his chest. Dawn light gilded her straight hair, as if reminding him she was beyond his reach, even if for this brief time she shared herself with him.

Amelie deserved better. Far better than Jules, the man who'd seduced then betrayed her. The thought of him made Lambis clench his teeth in thwarted anger. But he was no better. She needed someone who'd stand at her side, supporting, protecting and loving.

Once Lambis might have been that man. But not now. He was a shell of the man he'd believed himself to be.

'Don't stop.' The words were a gentle breath across his bare chest.

'I woke you? I'm sorry. Go back to sleep.' She'd need it after the hours they'd spent awake through the night.

For answer Amelie stretched, arching her back and pressing her breasts against him. Her smooth thigh slid across his legs and inevitably his half erect shaft stirred.

Lambis tried to focus on the stack of work waiting for his attention. The recruitment drive in the US, the potential problem with the big job in Russia—

'But I'm wide awake.' His eyes snapped open as Amelie lifted her head. Something shifted hard inside his chest as her slightly unfocused gaze met his. Something that was more than lust, though that was part of it.

Tenderness, desire and possessiveness surged in a potent mix he hadn't a hope of stopping, though it scared him witless. He hadn't felt anything so profound since—

'Lambis? Are you all right?'

Amelie's hair was a rumpled halo, her lips a sultry pout that was too enticing for a man trying to do the decent thing and rein in his apparently unstoppable libido. She must be sore after last night yet Lambis found himself stroking her supple flanks, letting his touch dip to explore her breasts.

Instantly those bright eyes glazed with a heat that matched the fire stirring in his loins.

'Very all right,' he growled.

And Amelie, the precious Princess he'd once thought as cosseted and delicate as a porcelain figurine, leaned up and whispered in his ear exactly how she'd like to celebrate the new day.

Seconds later she was on her back beneath him, smiling as he settled between her thighs. Ruthlessly Lambis banished his troubled conscience and focused on giving them both what they so desired.

'This was a brilliant idea, Lambis.' Amelie grinned and sat back beneath the vine-covered pergola. Dappled sunlight played across her features, already obscured by the dark glasses she'd insisted on wearing for their excursion into the village. 'I'm glad you persuaded me it was safe to come.'

'I wouldn't have suggested it if I hadn't known you'd be safe from the press.' He shrugged. 'I'm glad you like it. It's very simple.'

'But lovely.' Her gesture took in the plain wooden tables and rush-bottomed chairs in the small outdoor space where they were now the only customers, and the small harbour a few steps away. 'Even the boats are picturesque, and the colour of the water.' She sighed and leaned back, sipping her tiny cup of coffee. 'No wonder you wanted to have your home on the island.'

Ridiculous, but Lambis felt his smile grow at her enthusiasm. To many he knew, the quiet, unspoiled island would be too unsophisticated, too boring.

Amelie seemed to thrive on it. As for excitement, the closest she got were nights in his bed as he devoted himself to her. Nights filled with such potent pleasure he was hooked on the thrill of watching Amelie gasp out her completion in his arms, her beautiful eyes wide with awe. And, of course, to the rapture he himself found with his generous, sensual lover.

Lambis even felt a proprietorial pleasure at the way she'd developed a taste for Greek coffee, strong, short and pungently aromatic. And the way she'd eaten the plain village fare, with an easy relish that endeared her to the few locals who'd nodded their greeting.

He'd always known Amelie was genuine, but previously he'd only seen her in a royal setting, in that fanciful pale pink and white palace surrounded by its perfectly manicured grounds. There she drank from crystal and finest porcelain, surrounded by treasured antiques. Today she'd laughed, licking her fingers as oil dripped from the bread she'd used to mop up her plate.

The woman he'd come to know here was disarmingly frank, genuine and easy to please.

'Lambis!'

He blinked, diverted from thoughts of the many ways he enjoyed pleasing her.

'What is it?'

'Look at Seb.' Her whispered excitement was unmistakable. He whipped his head round to where Seb viewed the small fishing boats drawn up along the harbour. Lambis had been keeping an eye on him until thoughts of Amelie, naked in his bed, distracted him.

His shoulders relaxed as he saw Seb nodding at another boy about the same age who was speaking to him.

'He *talked*,' Amelie murmured. 'To a stranger!'

Lambis was unprepared for the blast of relief and excitement that rocked him as Sébastien smiled and spoke to the other kid. 'Didn't I tell you he'd be okay?' Till now, the boy had spoken rarely and, despite his optimism in front of Amelie, Lambis had harboured fears about the child's full recovery. 'Those experts were right. He just needs time.'

Slender fingers closed over his, yanking his attention back to Amelie. 'Time and somewhere he feels safe and unpressured. *You've* provided that. Thank you.'

'It was nothing.' He hadn't done anything special. It was *she* who'd fought for her nephew's recovery, not him. 'Here he gets to practice his Greek.'

The kid understood not only his father's native French but his mother's Greek as well as English, which was St Galla's second language. Suddenly it struck Lambis that unless he took a hand, Sébastien would lose the Greek his mother had taught him.

'Perhaps he could come back to Greece occasionally.'

Amelie's smile widened and instantly Lambis's pulse quickened. 'What a wonderful offer. Thank you. I'm sure he'd love visiting your island again.' Her hand squeezed his. 'You two have a special bond and that's strengthened since we came here.' Lambis watched her expression still. 'One day you'll make a wonderful father.'

As quickly as that the bright day dimmed. His stomach hollowed and metallic despair filled his mouth.

Lambis yanked his hand free. He couldn't see Amelie's eyes for the dark glasses but he read her voice—warm and approving.

He shuddered in denial.

The old wellspring of pain erupted, drenching him in icy ripples. 'I'll never be a father!'

Amelie stared as Lambis's face transformed. That hint of an indulgent smile, just turning up the corners of his mouth, vanished as his lips flattened. His skin somehow pared back, leaving his proud features angular and harsh, those black brows angling down in a frown that was nothing short of forbidding.

Fear rose as suddenly as a summer squall and she snapped her gaze around to check Seb. He was fine, sitting a few metres away in the sun, intent on what looked like a game of marbles.

She pressed a palm to her racing heart, trying to quell anxiety.

'Lambis? Are you all right?' Stupid question. Of course he wasn't all right. He looked like he had when she'd turned up unannounced at his mountain home—ruthlessly distant. Except she could read him better now and what she saw spoke of pain.

'I'm sorry. I didn't mean to offend you.' Though how she had she didn't know. 'I don't expect you to act as a surrogate father to Seb.' Though, no matter how hard she tried, she hadn't been able to douse that fantasy of her, Seb and Lambis together. She forced a tentative smile. 'I just meant—'

'You don't need to explain. I'm not offended.'

Yet something had happened. It was there in the way Lambis sat, ramrod straight, where before he'd lounged, relaxed and happy. His stormy eyes avoided hers.

Pain sliced through her. This last week they'd grown closer. She'd thought he trusted her.

She'd imagined that because they shared their bodies...

'Good.' She forced a bright smile as she pushed her cup aside. 'I think it's time Seb and I—'

'Leave the boy. It will do him good being with another kid.' Lambis's voice was gruff. Then his eyes met hers and her shoulders slammed back in her seat at the force of his bleak expression. 'There's nothing wrong. I just...' He shook his head in a tiny, impatient gesture. 'I won't ever have children. Didn't Irini tell you?'

Amelie shook her head. 'Irini never gossiped.' Except to say Lambis had had a difficult past. Amelie had never imagined that referred to an inability to father children.

'Ah.' Lambis nodded and turned his attention to the boys playing nearby. 'I had a son once,' he said quietly, the words strung taut and low. 'And a wife too. But they died.'

Such simple, straightforward words. But the power of them sucked Amelie dry. She stared into

Lambis's lifeless eyes. They stared blindly back and she guessed he didn't see her but the family he'd lost. A great gulf opened up inside her. It was as if an unseen force ripped her apart.

'I'm so very sorry, Lambis.' She leaned towards him, feeling the terrible inadequacy of mere speech, but needing to express her sympathy.

He nodded briefly. 'It was a long time ago.' Yet obviously it haunted him. How could it not?

Amelie ached with the need to touch him, to put her arms around him and draw him close. Not as a prelude to sex, but to offer that most basic comfort, a human touch, a reminder that someone cared.

Now she understood a little that withdrawn look she'd witnessed in the mountains.

To lose both a wife and child—it must have been some terrible accident. Having just lost her brother and sister-in-law so suddenly, she had some concept of what Lambis was going through. But she couldn't begin to understand what it was like to lose a child and a life partner.

Amelie swallowed, the movement convulsive. She had no more words.

His eyes met hers and this time he focused on her, so intently she felt the blood rise in her cheeks. 'I could never go through that again. I'll never marry or have another child.'

Dumbly, Amelie nodded, mind racing. Was that why Lambis had rejected her before? It seemed likely, especially as they'd proved since how compatible they were.

So much made sense—his initial diffidence with Seb, never unfriendly but never actively encouraging the boy, until that day on the beach when he'd seen the extent of Seb's distress. She wondered if it also explained why Lambis had relegated that beautiful, moving icon of mother and child to a guest room where he wouldn't see it. How could he look at it and not remember all he'd lost?

She hadn't thought it was possible to feel more pain than she had recently, but she did. It welled like a high summer tide, washing away her fragile hopes.

But her pain was nothing to Lambis's. Impulsively she shoved her chair back and got up, reaching for his fist, clenched so tight it quivered in her hold.

'Come on, Lambis. Let's walk. You promised to show us the little chapel at the end of the harbour.' Anything, surely, was better than watching him brood over the past.

She couldn't wipe away his hurt but she could at least distract him.

Beyond that, she could only share with him all the tenderness she felt until it was time for her and Seb to leave.

That would be the toughest part, she realised as Lambis got to his feet, his hand still in hers. For as he towered over her, that awful blankness still masking his features, Amelie realised something she'd gone to enormous lengths to avoid thinking about.

She loved Lambis Evangelos.

She'd never stopped loving him.

And while his heart was held by a dead woman there was no chance he'd come to love her.

CHAPTER TWELVE

'YOU'RE SURE THERE'S nothing wrong, Enide?' Amelie stared from Lambis's bedroom to the matchless view of sea and sky and perfect crescent beach. What was it about this conversation with her elderly relative that concerned her? She couldn't put her finger on it.

'Everything's under control. Now go and relax. And give Seb a cuddle for me. I'm so pleased to hear he's speaking again.'

'Not very much though.' Amelie bit her lip, wondering if she should risk returning with him to St Galla yet. Since hearing Lambis's story she couldn't help but suspect being around Seb was too close a reminder of the child he'd lost. 'Perhaps, after all, in his own home—'

'No!' Enide's vehemence surprised her. 'No, stay where you are a little longer. Why risk his recovery when he's doing well in Greece? Give the poor child time to recuperate. You could do with a longer break too.'

Enide's words made sense, yet Amelie couldn't shake the instinct that something was awry. 'Enide, I—'

'I'm sorry, Amelie. I really need to dash or I'll be late for a function. We'll talk later, yes?'

Before Amelie could respond, the line went dead, leaving her pondering. Her elegant, super-organised cousin Enide never dashed. She was never late. She was a stickler for punctuality and protocol, hiding her kind heart behind a cool exterior.

Amelie considered ringing back, but surely, if something was wrong, Enide would tell her. She'd been a brick, her quiet presence steadying Amelie when her whole world shattered.

'Everything okay?' Lambis's low voice encircled her as he entered the room. His arm slid around her waist from behind and instantly she melted against him, her pulse notching faster.

How long could she hide her feelings? It was a wonder he hadn't guessed. Every time they made love her passion held a dimension she knew was reserved solely for him.

Even the knowledge he still loved his wife and could never care for Amelie in that way hadn't changed her feelings. If anything, in the past days her love had strengthened, even as she told herself she needed to pull back.

But how could she when she craved his touch? When he was tender and gentle, passionate and demanding in ways that attuned so perfectly to her own needs? How could she when she understood his hurt and wanted to wrap him in her love, bringing him what solace she could, even knowing she couldn't heal him?

'I think so.'

'You don't sound sure. What can I do to help?'

Amelie turned in his embrace, delighting in this closeness, aware this must end soon. She had to make the break, though it seemed sometimes as if Lambis needed her as much as she needed him. His loving was so intense, so hungry… Which, she realised, was simply wishful thinking.

His grey eyes surveyed her seriously. He *would* help if he could. Without even knowing what that might involve.

What would he say if she admitted she loved him and what she needed was for him to let go of the past and love her?

Amelie sank against his chest, unable to resist temptation, and smiled, a tight, hard little smile as he pulled her close, one sinewy arm wrapped around her back and the other palming her hair in a familiar caress.

'Nothing. Everything's fine, Lambis.'

It scared her how adept she'd become at lying.

He should be working. Lambis felt the restlessness of a man who habitually devoted all his energies to business, yet who suddenly found himself distracted, neglecting his routine.

Yet, as his managers assured him, business was booming and, because of the structures and excellent staff he'd introduced, his company ran almost autonomously without micromanagement. Which meant he could take time out.

Face it. The business is all but running itself. You're just looking for an excuse not to be here.

Here being the ancient olive grove on the hill behind the villa, watching Amelie, in another of those wispy sarongs, and Sébastien explore the stony ground, intent on some insect they'd discovered.

The restlessness wasn't because Lambis wanted to be at his desk or on the phone. It was because Amelie and Sébastien had become integral to his days. Lambis found himself deciding certain matters he'd always handled could be delegated. He spent more time out of his office and even when he worked his thoughts turned to them—Sébastien, whose reserve was gradually disappearing, and Amelie. Above all, Amelie.

Lambis shifted his shoulders against the wide trunk of an old tree where he sat amongst the debris of their picnic.

His eyes narrowed on the remarkable woman who was as much at home in a filmy blue sarong and bare feet as she was in a full-length gown and tiara. Amelie couldn't be pigeonholed and she continued to surprise him. It had been days since he'd mentioned that he'd had a wife and child but Amelie hadn't once prodded for more details. She'd accepted the information with characteristic compassion but there'd been no interrogation.

Strangely, as the days passed, and the precious nights when Amelie shared herself ardently, making him feel more alive than he had in years, Lambis almost *wished* she'd ask.

He couldn't fathom it. He never talked about Dimitri and Delia. Ever.

Yet with Amelie more than once he'd been on the verge of talking about them. Like now as she stumbled her way through an old Greek rhyme Irini must have taught Sébastien. The boy was teaching Amelie and they giggled over her mistakes.

The rhyme, the laughter, the balmy air of the old orchard, reminded him of a day he'd forgotten till now, of Delia with Dimitri chanting the same rhyme.

Instinctively Lambis braced for the lancing agony that accompanied such memories. Instead, to his surprise, there was poignant sadness but it was swamped by gratitude that he had that memory. Gratitude for the years he'd had with them both.

Lambis's mouth firmed to a hard line. It wasn't right. He didn't deserve *not* to feel pain. It was because of him——

'Lambis.' Amelie's voice broke through his thoughts and he looked up to see her and Sébastien approaching, hand in hand. For a second, looking into the light, he couldn't make out her blonde hair. She could have been another woman, straight dark hair down around her shoulders, and a wide smile filling his heart with joy.

Lambis's breath caught. Then Amelie and Sébastien were standing before him and his vision cleared. Yet his lungs wouldn't work and guilt smote deep in his chest, cleaving right down to his belly.

What was she doing to his memories of Delia?

What was *he* doing to them?

He surged to his feet, heart thundering. It was only as Sébastien stared up in consternation that he realised how abruptly he'd moved. Tentatively he reached down and rumpled the kid's hair. But it was beyond him to force a smile.

'Sorry,' he said, his voice rougher than intended. 'I missed what you said.'

Amelie's smile had a fixed quality that told him he hadn't concealed his turmoil. Deliberately he wiped his face clear, an art he'd perfected not just in his years as a bodyguard, but as a man grieving the loss of everything that had made his life worth living.

'It's not important. It was just a bit of nonsense that can wait.' She glanced down at her nephew then back to him, her fine, arched eyebrows flattening. 'What's important is that Seb and I were talking about keeping up his Greek. I told him you'd help him with that in future. He'll always be able to count on you, like he can count on me. Right?'

Lambis knew what he had to say, what the boy needed to hear. Yet the idea of the lad *counting* on him turned that ache in his belly into a sharp slash of pain that threatened to undo him.

He cleared his throat but the words stuck in his throat. The worst thing the boy could do was count on him. That knowledge ate at Lambis.

He heaved a deep breath and nodded, planting his hand on Sébastien's shoulder. 'Of course you can. I'm your godfather after all.' He gave the bony little shoulder a gentle squeeze then stepped away.

'I'm afraid you'll have to excuse me. There's something I need to attend to.' Not meeting Amelie's eyes, he turned and marched back to the house. All the way his conscience, what was left of it, tormented him. It was dangerous to let the child think Lambis would be around to protect him. But what else could he have done?

He could only hope once Sébastien grew up, under the nurturing care of his aunt, he'd never need Lambis again.

'Do you want to talk about it?'

'Talk about what?' Lambis realised too late he shouldn't have agreed to this moonlit stroll by the sea with Amelie.

All evening she'd watched him, masking her scrutiny with smiles and light conversation. But he knew he'd worried her today. She'd been trying to allay Sébastien's fears about being left alone by reassuring him that she and Lambis would always support him. Lambis had done a poor job, though he'd done his best.

A spark of gallows humour flared. Since when had his best been good enough?

'About whatever's hurting you.' She didn't look at him, but kept up a steady pace as they walked the curve of the beach. 'Something is wrong. I want to help.'

'There's nothing anyone can do to help.'

He saw her face swing round and realised he'd just confirmed her suspicions.

'Sometimes talking can ease the burden.'

His mouth tightened. Nothing could ease what he felt, nor should it. Yet Amelie deserved to know, for didn't she look to him to support Sébastien? He couldn't let her raise unrealistic expectations.

'You told your nephew he could count on me.' That awful metallic taste was back in his mouth. 'But it's better not to let him think I'll be around to protect him.'

Her steps faltered. 'You're planning on deserting him?'

Lambis shook his head. 'No. But neither of you should rely on me. It's not wise.'

Not wise? It was too late to be wise where Lambis was concerned.

Amelie stopped as he turned to face the moonlit sea. How could she and Seb pull back now? They cared for and, yes, relied on him. Had she done wrong, bringing Seb here?

'I'm not good at protecting people.' A laugh emerged, but it sounded hard, a thing of pain, not humour. 'Ironic, isn't it, for a man who runs a security firm?'

Amelie stood silent, waiting.

'I can organise protection for complete strangers, but when it's people I care for...' His words trailed off and in the silvery light she saw his jaw tighten. 'I should have been able to protect Irini. I *should* have. I'd just done a security audit for the palace, after all.'

'You couldn't have saved her. You weren't even there.'

Lambis swung round to face her. 'But I'd seen the way your brother drove his previous boat and I knew about the powerful new racing one he'd ordered. He was good, but not that good. It was beyond his capabilities. I warned him that he needed proper training from a professional before using it.'

'I didn't know.' Amelie was stunned. Lambis was right about Michel at the wheel of a boat. He'd loved speed, loved cutting a course fine. 'But he'd never take risks with Irini!'

Lambis seemed not to hear. 'I think he took my advice as an insult. He certainly didn't thank me for it.'

Amelie could imagine that. 'He'd spent all his

life being told how to behave by older men. Even when he became King our Prime Minister tried to shackle him.' And Michel had been headstrong, a little impatient. But not reckless.

'I told Irini not to go out with him till he had some instruction. I should have made her promise. I should have made *him* see.' Lambis's voice was taut with regret, making Amelie remember her sister-in-law's hesitation to go out that day. Had she been recalling Lambis's advice?

'No one forced Irini to go with him.' Amelie stepped in front of Lambis. He refused to look at her. 'It was *her* decision. They were two adults and you had no way of stopping them.' She touched his hand, sliding her fingers through his and curling them tight. 'I saw them that day. He was going fast, but not recklessly. It was an accident. It's not your fault.'

Lambis shook his head, his features grim.

Amelie tugged at his hand. 'Michel adored her. He would never endanger Irini. It was an *accident*.'

But her words, instead of soothing, seemed to inflame. His fingers returned her grip with a strength that made hers tingle. His mouth flattened into a harsh slash.

'Lambis?'

Finally his gaze lowered. Even in the moonlight his pain was clear. So clear it jammed her breath tight in her lungs.

'I know what I'm talking about, Amelie. Love is

no protection. I loved my wife and son. But they're dead because of me.'

Amelie heard her breath hiss at the self-hatred in his voice, at the bitter twist of his mouth and, above all, the hurt in his eyes.

'I can't believe you did anything to endanger them, Lambis.'

It was true. The man she knew was strong, honourable, with a protective streak a mile wide. That protective instinct had overcome his need for solitude and his aversion to spending time with Seb. An aversion, she now guessed, that had nothing to do with Seb, but with Lambis's grief for his son. The way Lambis and Seb interacted now proved Lambis was a man with a profound capacity for caring. He was generous and gentle, and—

'Believe what you like. But it's true. Those close to me suffer.' His mouth twisted. 'In the old days they'd have said I was bad luck from the first, since my mother died giving birth to me.'

'What utter nonsense!' Amelie clutched both his hands, anger welling. 'That wasn't your fault.'

He shrugged. 'Delia and Dimitri, they were my fault.'

Delia and Dimitri. She hadn't heard their names before. 'What were they like?' she whispered.

Lambis's mouth turned up in a crooked smile. 'I fell in love with Delia when I was sixteen but we waited to marry until we had some money behind us.' His gaze took on a faraway look but Amelie guessed he wasn't seeing the silvered bay over her shoulder.

'Delia had a laugh that always made those around her smile and she had a kind word for everyone. Dimitri looked just like her—straight black hair, dark, merry eyes and that grin… He'd hare around the place at top speed, so full of energy.'

'He sounds like a lovely little boy.' And so like Seb had been before the accident—full of life and laughter. As for Delia, Amelie felt her heart hammer in sympathy for Lambis. Clearly he'd been head over heels in love with his wife. To Amelie's shame there was also possibly a tinge of jealousy. Because Lambis would never talk of *her* with such love in his voice.

What was it like to be so loved? Not for your position or title but for yourself? Loved by Lambis Evangelos, a man who committed himself totally and unswervingly to whatever he did?

Mentally Amelie gave herself a shake. This wasn't about her; it was about Lambis and the family that had been ripped from him. She squeezed his hands, sliding her thumbs over his, hoping the unspoken contact might ease just a tiny fraction of his grief.

'What happened to them?'

She felt a shudder pass through him, saw his jaw tighten. In the dark he looked like some carved sentinel, forbidding yet so boldly alluring it was impossible to look away from him.

'It was winter and we were staying in the mountains. There was a problem with a big new contract and I took the helicopter to Athens for a meeting.' He shook his head. 'I should never have gone. I had staff who could deal with it but I was so used to taking all the major decisions myself, managing every aspect of the business as it expanded...'

The raspy cadence of his voice tore at Amelie. She felt his desolation with a strength that only someone who'd experienced grief could understand.

'What we didn't know was that Dimitri was severely allergic to nuts. Anna said later that he went into anaphylactic shock. It would take too long for medical help so Delia bundled him into the car while Anna made the emergency calls. But Delia's car was at the mechanic's and there was only mine in the garage. She wasn't used to driving such a powerful vehicle, especially in snow.'

He pulled his hands from Amelie's as if he couldn't bear to be touched and Amelie felt part of her own heart crumble at his distress.

'They went off the side of the mountain road on a bend.' He paused, his breath labouring. 'The authorities said it would have been quick, almost instantaneous.'

'Oh, Lambis!' Amelie reached for him, then

stopped herself. Clearly he didn't want to be touched. 'I'm so very sorry. That was such a tragic thing to happen.'

'And avoidable.' His voice reminded her of broken glass. Or maybe it was the tightness in her own throat as she tried to swallow. 'Worse, it was my fault. Persuading Delia to live in such an isolated spot, just because my family had once lived there. Leaving them both alone instead of letting someone else handle the meeting.'

'You weren't to know that. You're not to blame, Lambis. No one knew about your son's allergy.'

He shook his head. 'I should have been there. If I'd been there with the chopper, things would have been different.'

'Everyone feels like that after a tragedy, but you're not to blame. No one could have known what would happen that day.' She paused, but he didn't seem to hear her. Amelie grabbed his arm. 'Don't you think I've thought again and again of how different things would have been if I'd suggested to Michel that he not take the boat out but spend the afternoon ashore instead?'

Lambis didn't respond. 'You can't keep thinking that way, Lambis. You'll go crazy.'

'Don't you see? They were my responsibility and I failed them. Just as I failed Irini.'

His utter implacability scared her. And angered her. 'You're not God, you're not omnipotent! You're just a man, Lambis, and you can't blame yourself for things that are totally out of your control.' She shook his arm, till he looked down at her. 'All you can do is pick up the pieces and move on as best you can. Anyone who loved you, like your wife did, would be horrified to think of you racked with guilt for something that wasn't your responsibility.'

Still no reaction from him. It shredded her heart, seeing him like this and being unable to reach him. She let go her hold and stepped back.

'Wallowing in the past is easier than facing the present or the future. It's self-indulgent, Lambis, especially when there are people who need you *now*.' Like Seb. And her. 'Do you really think Delia would want to see you like this? Anyone who loved life the way you say she did, would expect you to move on and keep living.'

Had she gone too far, invoking his wife's name? Yet Amelie had to try. The sight of Lambis bound in that tight web of guilt, unable to move on, unable to do anything but blame himself, was heart-wrenching.

Finally, when he remained silent, she withdrew her hand, to walk silent and alone to the house.

She had her answers. To why Lambis cut himself off. Why he'd avoided Seb, and rejected her. He had no room in his heart to love again.

Yet surely it was something close to love she'd seen as he interacted with Seb? Or maybe that was just a shadow of what he'd felt for his son.

As for coming to love her... She had a better chance of flying to the moon than seeing him turn to her with love in his eyes.

'Amelie?' Lambis's voice reached her across the gloom of his bedroom.

She shifted, leaning up on one elbow to watch him stride across the room and plant his feet beside the bed they'd shared for the last couple of weeks.

'I didn't think you'd be here.' She heard something in his tone that made everything in her still. Surprise, hesitance and...hope. It was the last that gave her courage. After all, her first instinct had been to sleep in her guest bedroom. Yet she couldn't bear the thought of leaving him, even though she'd given him solitude on the beach.

She pushed her hair back over her shoulder and tried to read his face. 'You want me to leave?'

'No! No, I'm just surprised.'

'You thought I'd turn my back on you?' Maybe she should have. Tonight had made it clear she had no hope of Lambis ever feeling for her as she did for him. He was a one-woman man, racked with guilt over his family.

'I didn't know. You sounded angry.'

She saw his hands tighten then unclench at his sides as if he were restless, suppressing powerful emotions.

Amelie shrugged, surprised to find he was right. Anger at the pointlessness of it mixed with regret and a deep, abiding sadness. 'I hate to see you torturing yourself this way. You have so much to offer, Lambis. So much to give.' She took a slow, steadying breath. 'One day I hope you find someone who'll help you realise that. Someone worth taking a risk for.'

Though it wouldn't be her, Amelie sincerely hoped one day the right woman would help Lambis tear free of the miasma that shrouded him.

'I don't want to think about the future.'

He looked so proud and strong standing there, silhouetted by moonlight. As if he were unassailable. Yet Amelie remembered the raw ache in his voice as he spoke of his family, and saw his apparent self-control for what it was—a defence mechanism. Her heart turned over.

Amelie pushed aside the sheet and opened her arms. 'Then let's just concentrate on here and now.'

He wasn't interested in her love, would probably run a mile if he guessed. But she could give him comfort. A comfort she discovered she needed almost as much.

For one tremulous moment she held her breath, wondering if he'd reject her. Then, before she had time to process the thought, he was in her arms, pushing her back onto the bed, his hot breath at her throat, her jaw, her breasts as he pressed hungry kisses to her flesh. Callused, urgent hands scraped her thighs as he tugged her nightdress high, then left her to make short work of his clothes.

Lambis came to her, hard and so needy he trembled with it. So driven there was no time for his usual generous foreplay. Instead, after one purposeful caress that found her wet and eager, he slid his hands beneath her bottom, tilting her up to meet him and thrust home, sure and true as if that was where he belonged.

Amelie blinked back hot tears. That was where he *did* belong. At the heart of her, making them both whole.

She grabbed his shoulders, winding her legs around his hips and feeling him sink even deeper. *Home.*

Then there was no more thought as his mouth took hers and he found the powerful rhythm that bound them tighter and tighter together until, lips still locked and hearts pounding in tandem, they raced to the edge of the precipice and flew off into the stars.

CHAPTER THIRTEEN

SEB'S LAUGHTER RANG out from the pool, followed by the deep burr of Lambis's voice. Ordinarily that would have made Amelie smile, for the pair had forged a bond of affection that grew stronger every hour. Despite occasional tears and clinginess, each day Seb seemed a little more like his old self. And he was talking!

Lambis might berate himself for not protecting his son, yet despite the pain he'd revealed that night on the beach he hadn't withdrawn from Seb. Lambis was too protective, too caring for that. He'd no sooner hurt the little boy than he would intentionally hurt Amelie.

Yet it was too late.

She was already hurt in ways that couldn't be fixed, loving a man who'd locked himself away because, she guessed, he was afraid of caring. Losing his family had all but broken this powerful man. Lambis felt so deeply.

Shutting her eyes, Amelie forced her mind away from Lambis. Back to the calamitous new problem on her hands.

Wearily she pressed her hand to her forehead as she turned back to the computer screen. But there was no mistaking the effusive media piece.

King Alex of Bengaria was definitely in St Galla, staying in *her* home, ready to attend the gala celebration that Amelie had cancelled ages ago in a discussion with the Prime Minister. Monsieur Barthe had nodded, saying he understood Seb had to be her priority. He'd promised his staff would make the necessary arrangements to reschedule the event.

Heart hammering, Amelie tried to recall the original date of the event. This week surely? She clicked on another report, this time with photos.

The world stopped.

Amelie blinked, trying to clear her vision, but nothing could shift the photo before her. King Alex outside a scientific research centre in St Galla after an official visit. And at his side, looking just a little distracted, was Princess Amelie of St Galla!

Amelie pressed the heel of her hand to her chest, trying to stop her galloping heart leaping free. She blinked, reading and rereading the caption. But there was no sane explanation. She'd never met Alex. His visit was to be the meeting that would help her decide if she wanted to get to know him better with a view to matrimony.

This wasn't an old photo of her and the handsome Prince.

Which meant she had a lookalike. Another woman who looked like her, pretending to *be* her!

Amelie sank back in her chair, mind racing, her skin clammy as nausea rose.

It should be impossible that anyone could look so much like her. Yet as she stared at the screen it was evident this wasn't just a matter of makeup and a wig. The woman could have been her double. *Was* her double!

It was the weirdest feeling, staring at a photo of herself and realising the woman in the photo wasn't her. Was there some slight difference in the angle of her jaw? Maybe around the eyes? Or was that wishful thinking? An instinctive rejection of the idea anyone could pass as her double? It was hard to tell but the other woman might be just a fraction shorter.

Which was neither here nor there. What mattered was finding out who she was and what she was doing taking Amelie's place.

Amelie had no close relations except Seb and Enide, the elderly second cousin who held the fort while she was away. So where did the unmistakable family resemblance come from?

Too easily her thoughts scrolled back to half-heard rumours about her father's infidelities. She'd been old enough to realise her parents hadn't had a happy marriage but she'd assumed the muted whispers were exaggerated. Now she wondered.

Taking a deep breath, Amelie reached for her phone and rang Enide.

Twenty minutes later, her head was spinning. She could barely believe what Enide had reluctantly admitted.

Far from cancelling King Alex's visit, the Prime Minister, Monsieur Barthe, had encouraged it, even having the temerity to tell Alex's staff she'd already *agreed* to a royal marriage! Barthe was set on her marrying a suitable husband, which in his old-fashioned reckoning meant a man with blood as blue as hers. Amelie ground her teeth, thinking of the lies he'd told. Of how he'd *used* her in his devious games.

Obviously Barthe thought he had her over a barrel with his threat to withhold the regency unless she married. As if she had to be a wife in order to be a mother to Seb!

Well, he had a fight on his hands. She'd always intended to dispute that. Now there was no way she'd bow to such pressure.

Plus he'd brought in a body double for her, a woman called Catherine or Cat Dubois. According to Enide, this Cat wasn't the go-getter she'd expected. Enide had taken a shine to her, which was rare since she was so protective of Amelie. True to form, Barthe had conned Cat as well. He hadn't told her King Alex would visit and she'd have to pretend to be Amelie with the man everyone now assumed Amelie would marry.

Not only that, but the public reception where they'd both appear was tonight! In just a couple of hours.

Amelie had no idea if she could get home by then. How long to fly to St Galla?

Lambis and Seb had disappeared so she'd called the housekeeper on the internal phone but she hadn't been able to tell Amelie if the helicopter would return today from the mainland.

Amelie pressed a hand to her breastbone, trying to still her racing heart. For, as if all that wasn't enough, Enide had other news too. Cat was Amelie's half-sister. She was the daughter of a maid who'd worked at the palace when Amelie's parents were first married.

Amelie swallowed bile at the idea of her father being unfaithful to her mother straight after their honeymoon. Disloyalty was anathema to her but that…

She'd always known her father was lazy and self-indulgent but she hadn't thought he'd stoop so low.

She shot to her feet, her emotions too turbulent to name. Except that deep within the roiling mess was excitement. She had a sister! That fact shone bright and hopeful.

How did you make the acquaintance of a sibling you hadn't known you possessed? A sibling who was doing her best to cover for you in difficult circumstances?

A sister she'd been deprived of all her life.

Amelie had learned it was best to live in the present, for everything could be snatched from you in an instant. She wouldn't give up Seb or put up with Barthe's machinations. She *would* get to know her sister. She might never have the love of the man who'd stolen her heart years ago, but there were other consolations in a life devoted to duty.

The phone rang. It would be Enide calling back as instructed. Amelie's blood ricocheted around her body so fast she reached out and grabbed the back of a chair.

She sank into it and reached for the phone. 'Hello? Enide?'

'Amelie? I can't tell you how sorry I am. I—' Enide sounded distraught.

'It's okay, Enide. This isn't your fault.' No, it was Prime Minister Barthe's for bullying her elderly relation into keeping quiet about this ludicrous masquerade. Poor Enide had thought she was protecting Amelie and Seb, knowing they needed peace and quiet.

'Is she there?' Funny how Amelie hesitated to speak her sister's name. Enide had said the woman was likeable and engaging yet Amelie felt nerves flutter in her stomach.

'I have her here. Are you absolutely sure—?'

'I'm sure. I'm fine, truly, Enide. Worry instead about Barthe. Keep an eye on him. He's more dangerous than even I realised.'

'Yes, of course. I will. But please, take care of yourself.'

'Of course.'

Amelie heard muffled noise at the other end of the line then a new voice.

'Hello?' It was a woman about her own age, speaking with an American accent. Amelie's pulse sped.

'Ms Dubois?'

'Yes?'

'It's Amelie here. Princess Amelie.' Never had she been more grateful for the years of experience in dealing with challenging situations. Her throat almost closed with nerves and excitement but her voice sounded fine.

'Your Highness.' Cat's voice was husky. With shock? Or was that how she usually sounded?

'Amelie, please.' She paused, slicking her tongue around dry lips. This was so hard over the phone. She wanted to *be* there to meet her sister and sort out this tangled mess. 'May I call you Cat?'

'Of course.'

'Thank you.' Questions hammered her brain. All the things she should ask about King Alex and Barthe and the reception. How had her half-sister, with absolutely no experience of the palace, coped? 'Are you all right, Cat?'

'I'm sorry?'

'I asked if you're okay.' Amelie sighed, drawing the hair back from her face with trembling fingers. How she wished Lambis were here. He'd tell her if she could get to St Galla tonight.

'I've just found out about this scheme for you to take my place at tonight's reception. I had no idea. The event should have been cancelled when I told the Prime Minister I wouldn't be there. I believed it *had* been cancelled.' Her mouth tightened at the prospect of confronting Barthe. He might run the nation but he'd learn he didn't run her!

'I haven't been watching the news, you see, and I haven't been in regular contact with anyone at the palace.' Except Enide, who'd known she was at her wits' end trying help Seb. 'So I didn't know you'd been brought in. Are you all right?'

'I'm fine. I…well, I'm not very good at being a princess, but I'm muddling through.'

Despite her tension, Amelie smiled. She admired how Cat downplayed what must have been a massive challenge. Maybe they did have some things in common. 'Even with King Alex in the palace?'

There was no answer.

'Cat? Are you sure you're all right?' Concern tinged her voice. Crazy to be worried about someone she didn't know existed till now, but there it was.

'I'm fine. And Alex knows the truth. He guessed some time ago.'

'Yet he's still there?' Amelie couldn't hide her astonishment. She'd heard only good things about Alex, which was why she hadn't rejected the marriage idea instantly. But why hadn't he left St Galla when he'd realised he was being duped?

'He knows it's not your doing. He blames Monsieur Barthe. But he's willing to go along with the pretence so there's no public scandal.' Cat paused. 'But there's something else you need to know. He made it clear, even before he found out who I was, that he wasn't interested in marriage.'

Amelie slumped back in her chair. 'Thank God. That's one thing less to worry about.'

'You're pleased?' Cat was confused.

'I agreed to entertain the idea, but my heart wasn't in it.' Amelie's laugh was bitter. Now wasn't the time to dwell on where her heart *was* engaged.

'Are *you* all right? I've been worried you might be in trouble.'

'That's kind of you.' Amelie felt a rush of warmth for this stranger who didn't feel like a stranger. 'Things haven't gone quite as I'd expected but I'm coming home.' She'd put that off too long, hoping to reach Lambis at more than a physical level. As if somehow she could *will* him to love her. How pathetic was that? Amelie straightened. 'I'd like, very much, to meet you. I…' She paused, struck anew by the depth of her emotions. 'I didn't know you existed till Enide told me.'

'I'd like that.' Amelie heard the emotion in Cat's voice too.

'Good. I'm looking forward to it too.' Amelie forced herself to focus on the tangled mess in St Galla. 'Now, about tonight. I'll see if I can get there in time. Transport is a bit limited from here and—'

'It's all right. I can do it. It's only for a couple

of hours and with Enide and Alex watching out for me I'll be fine.'

'Alex?' The way Cat said his name intrigued her.

'He's been...helpful.'

'I see.' Amelie paused, frantically trying to calculate the most sensible way forward. Was it better for both of them to be in St Galla tonight, assuming she could get transport? Or safer to stay away till after the reception so there weren't two princesses in the same place? Enide had said Cat was leaving tomorrow. 'Are you absolutely sure? I couldn't guarantee I'd get there exactly on time but—'

'I'm sure. I'll manage. I'm sure you have other things on your mind than tonight's reception.' There was a pause. 'I hope Prince Sébastien is well.'

'He's fine.' Despite everything, Amelie smiled. No matter what scandal they courted with this charade in St Galla, Seb was on the mend. *That* was what mattered. 'Much better than before.'

'Amelie?' Lambis's deep voice made her turn in her seat. He stood, filling the doorway, and inevitably her heart gave that little shimmy of delight.

She pressed her hand to her chest. She *had* to move on. She couldn't continue like this.

Amelie turned away from the door. 'I'm sorry. I have to go. Are you sure about tonight? I can try—'

'Absolutely.' The certainty in her sister's voice

convinced her. Amelie sat back, surprised at the relief filling her. She'd have to deal with Monsieur Barthe and King Alex, but not till tomorrow. She was used to being the one who managed, who kept everything running, who took responsibility. It was a novel thing to relinquish control to another.

As she had with Seb, she realised, letting Lambis help shoulder the burden of responsibility and care.

'Thank you, Cat. If you can manage tonight it will give me a little time to…organise things. But we'll talk soon and arrange to meet, either in St Galla or elsewhere.'

Amelie was surprised her hand didn't shake as she put the phone down. When she looked up Lambis stood before her. He was so unnaturally still she sensed his hyper-alertness. What did he read in her face?

She looked away, telling herself it didn't matter what he read, or how he reacted. Lambis had made it clear he had no place in her future, except as an occasional visitor to Seb. It was time to move on.

'What's happened? What's the problem?' His voice was terse, that of a man used to taking charge in difficult situations.

Well, he wouldn't have to deal with this. She'd handle it alone.

It was time to say goodbye.

Pinning on a smile, she met those piercing eyes, ignoring the way her heart fluttered. 'It's time Seb and I went home.'

Home? Shock jerked his body. Lambis had guessed it when his housekeeper relayed the query about the chopper. But hearing Amelie say it...

It was a measure of the change she'd wrought in him that, instead of being relieved at the prospect of solitude, Lambis wanted to wail and gnash his teeth. More, he wanted to wipe that polite smile off her beautiful lips with a kiss that would turn her compliant and eager in his arms. He wanted her to say she wouldn't leave him.

His head reared back.

'Leaving? You can't go yet. Seb's not fully recovered.'

Her smile looked strained but she didn't turn away. 'I suspect that will take a long time, for both of us.'

What was she saying? That he'd taken advantage of her grief?

She was right. Where Amelie was concerned he hadn't any restraint—possibly because he'd been keeping his distance for years. His resistance to her had finally eroded.

'Seb's talking, which is a start. It will be enough for the upcoming ceremony, so his future will be secure. That's what matters.' Her gaze left his and he found himself bereft. Adrift like an unmoored boat.

Had he expected her to say *they* mattered? That together they'd created a bond that couldn't be ignored?

He was the one who'd warned her he couldn't commit.

He sensed he was already losing her. Her thoughts were in St Galla.

For an insane moment Lambis wanted to grab her chin and pull her face round to his, make her look him in the eye and admit they were—

Nothing. They were nothing. She wasn't for him.

Yet the prospect of her leaving hurt more than he'd thought possible.

'Why do you need to go? What's happened?'

She shrugged. 'It's a long story.'

Lambis folded his arms. 'I have time.'

That made her look up. Green eyes met his and he leaned closer, inevitably drawn by the unguarded confusion he read there.

'Amelie—'

'It's all a mess.' She spoke quickly. 'Monsieur Barthe was supposed to cancel an official visit by King Alex of Bengaria. I told him to reschedule it but he hasn't. The King is there now and...' She shook her head. 'It's complicated.'

'Alex of Bengaria?' Lambis's firm had done work in Bengaria. He remembered the King—

decisive, approachable and, according to Lambis's female staff, utterly irresistible.

Lambis's gaze narrowed on the woman before him, looking so ill at ease. 'He's the royal they want you to marry?'

She started at his harsh tone, then nodded. 'Yes. But it's unlikely now.'

Lambis barely heard her over the rush of blood filling his head. '*That's* what's so important? You're rushing back to be with *him*?' He grimaced at the bitter taste in his mouth.

'There's no need to look like that. There are complications I need to sort out.' Amelie got to her feet, staring at him as if she'd never seen him. Or perhaps comparing him to the polished, pretty-boy Prince waiting for her in St Galla.

Something dark and feral stirred in Lambis's soul. Something he didn't recognise. It was angry, wanting to lash out, but hurting too. Of course Amelie would choose to be with another blue-blood, instead of a reclusive man with working class roots. He had no right to feel indignant. He'd told her time and again she couldn't rely on him long-term. Alex, on the other hand, was apparently ready for marriage.

He owed it to Amelie to shut up and let her walk away.

'You'd really give yourself to him?' The thought of Amelie in another man's arms, in his bed, all but broke him. He felt as if his ribs were caught in a vice that screwed tighter and tighter.

Amelie frowned and Lambis wanted to kiss her brow smooth, stroke her cheeks, tease her lips till she opened for him.

'I told you, it's unlikely.' Her chin tilted with a hauteur designed to freeze him on the spot, but which instead made the fire in his belly burn even brighter.

'You deserve better than someone who doesn't even *care* for you. You tried that with Jules, and you got hurt.' She'd tried to hide that but she wasn't as adept at concealing emotion as she thought. Besides, Lambis knew her now. He understood that however strong she was, Amelie was a woman with heart. She loved and deserved love in return.

'You need someone who'll fight for you. Not someone who views you as a convenient spouse.' His words spilled out, harsh and overloud.

Lambis could never be the man she wanted. Yet he couldn't stand by while she threw herself away on a man who'd ultimately destroy her. However good his intentions, Alex's indifference would eventually kill a woman who was clearly designed for love.

'Well.' Her eyes glittered gem-bright, her nostrils flaring as she dragged in air. 'If ever you find such a man, be sure to tell me. I've yet to find one.' Her eyes flashed like daggers. He felt the sharp prick of that look at his heart. Guilt drove into him like a sharpened spike through soft flesh. For, of course, it wasn't just Jules who'd let her down. It was Lambis too.

He couldn't reconcile his no-emotional-entanglements attitude with this urgent need to keep her here and convince her Alex wasn't the man for her.

He couldn't offer what she wanted, yet he didn't want anyone else getting close to her.

'Now, is it possible to use your helicopter? I want to return to St Galla tomorrow. I'll pay, naturally, and—'

'Don't!' What she heard in his voice, Lambis didn't know. He only knew he was closer to doing something utterly reckless than he'd been in all the years since he'd lost Delia and Dimitri. He hefted in a draught of oxygen. 'I'll take you. Leave everything to me.'

Hours later, with every detail of the trip sorted and his schedule cleared, Lambis slowly walked back from the beach. He hadn't seen Amelie since dinner, where their conversation had been stilted, like a couple of chance met strangers, picking their way through neutral topics.

He hated the distance between them. The invisible but real barriers Amelie had erected. Was that how it had felt for her when he'd pushed her away years before?

He shook his head, swearing under his breath. Everything felt wrong. Out of control. Nothing was as it should be. He didn't want Amelie and Sébastien to leave.

He didn't want to be alone.

Lambis slammed to a halt, heart pounding. Since when had solitude been anything but a balm?

Since Amelie and Sébastien had made him feel again.

He grimaced. It sounded so simple. If this were a movie he'd magically forget all the reasons he was a bad risk. Forget how he'd failed those he cared for. But he couldn't do that to Amelie. She deserved far better.

His throat and lungs ached as he drew in another, laboured breath.

He wanted her but couldn't, *mustn't*, have her. What he had to do was let her go.

He stood, swaying, forcing himself to face that unbearable fact.

Finally, his heart, his whole body aching, he followed the path up to the house and the French windows giving directly onto his room.

He'd deliver her to St Galla and he'd make it clear to this Alex that he'd have Lambis to deal with if he let Amelie down. He stepped into the dark room, mind fixed on that interview, when he realised he wasn't alone.

Amelie was in his bed.

His heart stalled as she sat up. The sheet fell away to reveal the sweet, proud jut of her breasts. Her hair cascaded around her shoulders like pale silk. Her eyes were unreadable in the shadows, but there was a vulnerability about the set of her shoulders and the too-high angle of her chin, almost as if she expected him to reject her.

It was all he could do not to sink to his knees in thankfulness.

That ache in his chest honed to a fixed point of sharp pain, a counterpoint to the razor-edge of desire slicing his belly.

Lambis wanted her so badly he could barely contain himself. He wanted her tenderness as well as her body. Her smiles, her...

He shoved aside thought, unable to cope with all he was about to lose when she returned to St Galla. Instead he paced to the bed, eating her up with his eyes.

Steadily she stared back as he tore at his clothes, flinging them aside. There was no doubt in her as she proudly faced him, only a certainty that humbled him.

Lambis pulled the sheet aside. Then he began worshipping her with his body, his heart and soul. He would give them both memories that would last long after she'd gone.

CHAPTER FOURTEEN

THEY ARRIVED THE next afternoon at a private airfield. Lambis had flown them via helicopter to the Greek mainland and organised the private jet and the anonymous car with heavily tinted windows that took them to the St Gallan palace.

He glanced at Amelie, on the other side of the limo's wide back seat. She was tense despite the bright smile she gave her nephew. 'Here we are, *mon lapin*, home again. Tonight you'll sleep in your own bed and before that you can play with all your toys.'

Sébastien nodded and cuddled his teddy bear close. He'd been quiet since they touched down.

'Perhaps you can show me the best place to swim here,' Lambis found himself saying. 'I haven't swum for so long!'

The boy giggled. 'But we swam yesterday.' Lambis saw Amelie's high shoulders relax a little at that giggle. Clearly she'd been worried too how her nephew would cope, returning to the palace with its memories.

'So I did. How silly of me to forget. Will you swim with me?' He kept the boy talking, giving Amelie time to harness her emotions. For despite her almost iron control he could read her now. Her tension had increased steadily all day. Or perhaps it was anger.

Finally, in the early hours, as they lay sated yet wide awake in each other's arms, she'd told him about the Prime Minister's audacious masquerade scheme. About the half-sister she'd yet to meet, and the increasing pressure being brought to bear on Amelie to marry.

At least that was one thing Lambis had been able to do for Amelie, tell her a little about Cat. For it had been Lambis who'd met her years before and recommended her to the St Gallan authorities in case a body double was ever needed for Amelie. He hadn't known they were half-sisters, just that they looked remarkably similar. And Cat had impressed him as honest, talented and likeable. If he'd known the Prime Minister would use his recommendation to deceive everyone in this way... Fury coursed through him.

But it was nothing to the other emotions haunting him.

Holding her in his arms, Lambis had felt a regret so poignant it unnerved him. For he had nothing to give that would keep her with him.

They'd both been conscious it was their last night together. It had been there in each caress and their quiet desperation as they shared themselves. As if neither wanted to face the dawn.

Now, knowing the enormity of what Amelie confronted, Lambis was determined to do whatever he could to help. For the moment that meant keeping Sébastien occupied and happy.

Lambis looked up as the limo turned into a wide gateway and drove sedately towards the fanciful *belle époque* palace. Its soft pink stone was decorated with white marble windows and doors that from a distance looked as delicate as frosting on a cake. Yet there was no mistaking it for anything but a seat of power, set in its own extensive gardens that occupied the whole southern tip of the island.

Minutes later they stood at the palace entrance, the scent of flowers mingling with the rich perfume of pines and the sea. Enide, the elderly relative Lambis knew from previous visits, was whispering to Amelie. The old woman's well-bred, slightly horsey face was creased with anxiety. As she spoke Lambis watched the last vestige of Amelie's animation flicker and die. She didn't frown but the smooth, expressionless mask of calm she adopted was worse.

The warm, sensual woman he knew was being buried beneath her royal burdens.

Lambis's hand tightened on Sébastien's as he fought the impulse to go to her. The urge to wrap his arms around both Amelie and Sébastien grew. He was accustomed to being there for them.

Someone else—a secretary?—joined the small, serious group and Amelie nodded, answering a question about an urgent meeting. Her voice was crisp and businesslike.

He wasn't surprised. Amelie was far more than a pretty face or a devoted aunt. She was capable and efficient.

She'd be fine.

Yet Lambis couldn't dispel the memory of her in his arms before dawn. How she'd trembled with indignation at the devious schemes of her Prime Minister. How her voice had been strained and her touch needy.

How she'd sighed her pleasure and given herself to Lambis utterly, no holding back. He'd felt for that too-brief interlude as if they'd both found peace. As if he'd found the missing part that completed him.

Lambis hunkered down beside Sébastien, asking him about the view from the palace. But as the little kid replied, more than half Lambis's attention was on Amelie. She was in control, no doubt of that, and more than capable. Yet he couldn't quench the emotions that wrenched at him, seeing her so alone, the weight of the kingdom, her nephew's wellbeing and now this fiasco with the Prime Minister on her shoulders.

'Seb? Shall we go in?' Her smile for the boy was the same as always. Only the shadows in her eyes were different. And the way she avoided looking at Lambis. His heart thudded dully in his chest cavity.

Then they were moving into the palace. Staff clustered and welcomed. Enide shook his hand, thanking him for all he'd done, which only made

Lambis recall how reluctantly he'd helped. Only after Amelie had forced his hand.

Lambis looked around the grand foyer, built to impress and intimidate. A huge chandelier dripped from the ceiling and the walls were hung with a collection of art that had left more than one connoisseur breathless. The place even smelled different. Rich, luxurious, refined.

This was Amelie's world, her home.

Yet he knew in his deepest self that she'd never been more alone than now. A vast ache pulsed within him.

'Wait!' His voice echoed around the vast space, too strident and peremptory. Faces turned.

Lambis turned to Sébastien. 'How about you go with your Aunt Enide? I'm sure Monsieur Bernhard wants to check out his old bed. Then I'll join you and we can swim together.'

Sébastien regarded him for a moment then looked at Bernhard, his bear. 'Okay. But don't be long.'

More than one person gasped, surprised the little Prince was speaking. But Lambis's attention wasn't on the attendants, it was on Amelie. 'We need to talk.'

'Later. I have to meet—'

'I know.' His eyes locked with hers over Sébastien's head. Lambis ignored the shocked glances that he'd dared interrupt the Princess. 'But first there's something you need to hear.' His heart beat a sharp, accelerating tattoo and his jaw clenched so hard pain radiated down his neck.

Finally she nodded and, with a hug for Sébastien and a couple of murmured words to the others, led the way down a wide hall into a salon.

Lambis closed the door behind them, watching Amelie pace to the window. The afternoon light limned her in gold, accentuating that aura of untouchability she'd donned along with her regal composure. She wore a skirt and jacket he hadn't seen before today, slim-fitting, in a soft green that matched the peridot earrings that swayed as she turned. Her only other jewellery was the familiar pearl and gold pendant but she couldn't be more breathtaking if she wore a whole treasury of royal finery.

His heart clenched then tripped to a quickening rhythm as he crossed the room. He pulled up as she raised her hand.

Gone was this morning's lover. Where before there'd been tenderness, now he read…nothing.

Even knowing this was a necessary tactic for Amelie to concentrate on the onerous tasks before her, Lambis silently railed at this change. He didn't want distance. He didn't want them to be strangers again.

'Marry me.' The words surged out, rough and urgent.

Her eyes widened and he thought she swayed on her delicate heels.

'Marry me, Amelie.' His voice was pure gravel. He swallowed hard, trying to clear the restriction in his throat. 'Let me help you.'

He moved closer though he kept his arms by his sides. If he touched her he wouldn't be able to keep the lid on the bubbling brew of emotions. The strain of keeping his distance reverberated through him, a discordant note.

'Help me?' Her face was pale, her nostrils flared as if she couldn't get enough air. One hand lifted to her pearl pendant then dropped away.

'Yes.' Another step closer, breathing in her entrancing scent, warm flesh and gardenias. His gaze dropped to her mouth with its delicate pink tint then to the little pulse at the base of her throat, tripping so fast. 'There's no need to marry a total stranger, like Alex of Bengaria.'

There's no need to sell yourself for your nephew's sake.

She was going to fight the Prime Minister for the right to be named Sébastien's Regent, but if she was unsuccessful...

The thought of Amelie in a stranger's bed was bad enough. The idea of her with someone who'd married her only for her status and ability to breed an heir left Lambis sick to the stomach.

He couldn't let that happen.

He took a deep breath and felt a sense of absolute rightness creep over him. 'You don't have to do this alone.' His voice was smoother now, the words coming more easily. 'Marry me. I can...' The word *protect* hovered on his tongue but he couldn't lie. 'I can help. Marry me and you'll be made Regent. Sébastien's future will be secure. You deserve to have someone who'll fight for you. Someone who knows and respects you.'

Amelie stared into those hooded grey eyes. She'd seen them dark as storm clouds as Lambis had thundered at her, trying to push her away. She'd seen them bright as summer lightning, their heat searing her as they made love and he lost himself inside her. She'd thought then that nothing could be more intense than that pinnacle of exquisite oneness, that oneness she'd known only with Lambis.

She'd been wrong. Looking into his serious eyes, reading the dreadful tension in his big frame, Amelie felt a pain so sharp it was as if someone had stabbed her through the heart.

Her poor, stupid, still hopeful heart that for one thrilling, heady moment had waited for Lambis to talk of love.

Amelie swallowed. Lambis had given his heart to his wife, Delia, and that was the end of it. It was Amelie's luck to fall head over heels for a one-woman man. A man who was strong, honest, loyal and caring, who was wonderful with Seb and made Amelie feel...

She blinked and shook her head. She didn't know whether to laugh or cry.

How she wanted to say yes. She actually had to bite her tongue to stop the words leaping out. Especially when she saw what this cost Lambis. His hands were clenched into white-knuckled fists and there was a repressed energy about him that she guessed came from the effort to stand there and make the offer he thought she wanted.

But it was so much less than what she needed.

'Thank you, Lambis.' Her voice wasn't her own. She paused, her gaze fixed on his face, though what she really wanted to do was swing away and give in to the hot tears pressing the back of her eyes. 'Thank you, but no.'

His flesh tightened on his bones, emphasising his strong features, as if he'd shrunk before her eyes. But he was still utterly imposing. Tall, powerful, chivalrous. He was trying to protect her even though he'd reasoned himself into believing he could protect no one. He was hardwired that way. He could no sooner ignore her plight than she could ignore the love for him that thrummed in her blood.

But what they couldn't change they could ignore. They had to.

Lambis opened his mouth to speak and Amelie hurried on, not trusting herself not to be swayed.

'It's a kind offer. I appreciate it.' She swallowed hard, tasting the salt tang of distress. 'I'm honoured that you respect me and I know without doubt you'd fight for me and for Seb, but...' One slow breath. Another. She clasped her hands before her, tight enough to hide the way they shook.

'But while I appreciate that, I want more. I don't want sacrifice, I want *love*. You had love once, so you know how important it is. I want… the chance to find that.' Her words petered out to a hoarse whisper. 'So thank you for your concern, and your offer, but I can't accept.' Amelie tugged in a swift, shallow breath, trying to mask crushing hurt. 'You'll always be welcome here. I know Seb loves you.' She halted the words on her tongue about how *she* loved him too. 'And I hope you'll always be part of his life.'

Lambis stared unblinking, as if she'd dealt him a stunning blow. Pain seized her at the hurt she'd inflicted. Until she reasoned it wasn't hurt. Maybe Lambis's pride was bruised at the rejection.

'Now, I'm sorry, but I really must go. I have to meet King Alex and the Prime Minister.'

Amelie bit back a mirthless smile. Facing the bullying Barthe and Alex of Bengaria, the man who'd been shamelessly lied to ever since he'd set foot in her home, had seemed daunting an hour ago. Now that paled to insignificance in the face of rejecting a proposal from the only man she'd ever truly loved.

CHAPTER FIFTEEN

'THANK YOU AGAIN, ALEX. You've been unbelievably understanding.'

The man before her on the terrace shook his head, his deep blue eyes crinkling as he smiled. Truly, if she weren't pining for a man she could never have, Amelie could imagine falling for Alex of Bengaria. He had so many qualities she admired.

He just wasn't Lambis.

Her heart clenched and she had to force herself to breathe. She'd deal with the pain when she had the luxury of being alone.

'It wasn't your fault. You knew nothing about Barthe's machinations and Cat's masquerade.'

They'd spent the afternoon together, dealing with the Prime Minister and ensuring there was no fallout from Cat's masquerade as Amelie. More, between them, they'd made Barthe see he had no future leading the nation. They'd given him a choice—resign or have them expose his double dealing. He'd chosen to resign, and with his departure the opposition to Amelie as Regent lost its drive. Now, with Seb able to talk, the upcoming ceremony should be a mere formality.

It had been a long, exhausting few hours, but

the way ahead was brighter. If only Amelie could feel jubilant about it.

'I feel responsible. You'll go away thinking we St Gallans are liars and cheats.'

Alex shook his head. 'On the contrary, I've developed a soft spot for St Galla and its people.'

'And particularly for Cat?' It was none of her business, but discovering her half-sister Cat and Alex were close, and seeing his concern on learning Cat had already left for New York, she couldn't help wondering.

His smile disintegrated. 'Absolutely. But *she* doesn't think so. I was so busy racing off to confront your Prime Minister to scotch rumours about the pair of us, she left St Galla before I could talk to her. Now she's not answering her phone.'

Amelie reached out and touched his hand. 'Then follow her. Make her listen.' Her voice dropped. 'Love is too important to give up.'

His blue eyes narrowed. 'You understand, don't you?'

Amelie's instinct was to deny it. What was the point? Alex wouldn't tell anyone, and besides, the urge to confide was overwhelming.

'I do.'

She didn't say any more but Alex heard the hurt in her voice, or perhaps read her face. His hand turned to clasp hers. 'It's not something that can be worked out?'

Amelie's mouth tightened as familiar pain welled. 'Sadly, no. He's in love with someone else.'

'Ah. I'm sorry.'

For a moment they stood, unmoving and silent in the rich afternoon light. Then Amelie forced a lighter note. 'Can I persuade you to spend another evening here as my guest, or are you going to hot-foot it after my sister?'

Something flared in Alex's eyes and Amelie told herself Cat was one lucky woman. He was obviously head over heels in love.

'I'm not sure. I want to follow her but I suspect she's furious and won't listen. I may have to think of a better plan.'

Intrigued, Amelie was about to enquire further when she noticed someone coming towards them through the formal garden. A tall, imposing figure who moved with a casual grace that belied the strength in that massive form. Beside him skipped Seb, golden hair bright in the last rays of sunlight.

She stilled, willing herself not to feel anything and failing miserably.

Alex released her hand and turned to follow her gaze. When he turned back his expression was sympathetic. 'Actually, I think I'll leave now, if you don't mind?'

'Of course not.' She summoned a smile. 'Good luck with Cat. I'm hoping to visit her in New York soon.'

'If I'm successful, you may be visiting her in Bengaria instead.'

Amelie nodded. 'Good luck.' She liked and admired Alex and, though they'd never met, she already had a soft spot for her half-sister, Cat. She couldn't wait to get to know her properly. It would be wonderful if this pair could sort out their differences and find happiness together.

Alex took her hand and raised it to his lips. 'I'll hope to see you soon in Bengaria. No need to see me out. I suspect you have other important matters to deal with.'

Amelie stilled. There was nothing more to sort out. Seb's future was safe and her role as his guardian secure. As for Lambis... No, there was nothing more to be done.

Alex entered the palace and Amelie turned to follow. She didn't want a *tête-à-tête* with Lambis. But the sound of voices stopped her. Enide had approached down one of the gravel paths, meeting Seb and Lambis.

Then, before Amelie could move, Enide and Seb headed off together and Lambis strode directly towards her. His long legs ate up the distance at an alarming rate. In black jeans and a charcoal shirt that matched his eyes, and with his glossy hair falling over his brow, he looked deliciously ruffled and dangerously sexy.

Amelie's pulse fluttered, matching the butterflies in her stomach. Or were they swallows, swooping and dipping in dizzying aerobatics?

She made herself stand firm. Surely, after facing down her Prime Minister and the foreign King who'd been duped and deceived in her own palace, Amelie could face Lambis?

He was probably coming to say he was leaving. There was nothing to keep him now he'd brought her and Seb home. He must be relieved she hadn't clutched at his unwilling proposal.

Pasting on a gracious smile, she swung to face him fully, telling herself she wasn't in the least disconcerted by his aura of restless energy.

He stopped too near. So near instinct screamed she should retreat. Instead she widened her stance. This was her home. She'd be polite, wish him bon voyage and that would be it.

'You and King Alex? You came to an agreement?' Gone were the rich, deep tones she'd become addicted to. The soft burr of sound that had wrapped around her and soothed her into sleep more than once. Instead that bass voice was harsh, rough-edged.

'Sorry?'

'You touched him.'

Lambis stood before her, arms akimbo, those broad shoulders thrust back, accentuating the sheer masculine power of him. But it was the accusation in his tone that confused her.

Till understanding kicked in, then anger. He

didn't want love her, but he resented her touching another man?

Amelie folded her arms. 'I fail to see what that's got to do with you.'

'He kissed your hand.' It came out as a growl like the first warning roll of thunder before a violent electrical storm.

Instead of scaring her, that stoked her defiance. 'Again, none of your business.' She tried to freeze him with the haughty glare that had been her father's stock-in-trade.

Lambis ignored it, stepping in so she had to tilt her head back. But Amelie refused to back away. She'd had enough of men trying to tell her how to live her life.

'What if I make it my business?' There was no mistaking that aggressively proprietorial tone. Despite her anger, Amelie felt a thrill of feminine delight. Till she reminded herself this was dog-in-the-manger stuff.

'We've been over this, Lambis.'

Slowly he shook his head, his eyes never leaving hers. That was when the fiercely combative electricity between them changed. When she saw what was in those clouded eyes.

'Lambis?' Her voice cracked.

'Have you agreed to marry him? You let him *kiss* you.'

'Only my hand.' Amelie stared, her brain seizing at what she thought she saw in his face.

'You let him *kiss* you.' Large hands folded around her shoulders. He didn't pull her close, just held her, and to her amazement Amelie felt him shake.

She reached out. To push him away? Instead her hand settled on the solid heat of his chest. His heart pounded urgently beneath her palm. Her mouth dried.

'Don't do this, Amelie. He's not the man for you.'

'He's a fine, decent man.' Where the words came from, Amelie had no idea. Lambis was right—Alex wasn't for her.

'He won't make you happy.' Lambis's hands tightened on her shoulders.

'You can't know that.' How dare he act as if he knew what was best?

'I've never been more certain of anything.' Beneath her hand his massive chest rose with a shuddering sigh. 'You belong with me.'

Instantly Amelie stepped back, or tried to. Lambis stopped her.

This was too much to bear, too tempting for a woman in love, no matter how many times she'd told herself she deserved more than a convenient marriage for the sake of her nephew.

'Please let go, Lambis.' She swiped her tongue over lips grown suddenly parched, her gaze skittering away. She was deluding herself, imagining he felt—

'Never.'

Amelie's head jerked up in shock. But before she had a chance to speak he bent to her, his mouth settling on hers firmly, possessively, so sweetly she was sure she heard angels sing. His lips moved on hers, coaxing and enticing, so that when his tongue swiped the seam of her mouth it took no pressure at all for him to delve inside.

Lambis's kiss was tender but not tentative. It was the kiss of a lover coming home. A partner sharing pleasure. It undid her utterly.

'Ah, Amelie, *karthia mou*. Don't cry.' Gentle thumbs swiped her cheeks as he pulled back, resting his forehead on hers.

Her shoulders shook on a sobbing breath. She couldn't do this any longer, couldn't pretend.

'Forgive me, *agapi mou*. I can't bear to see you hurt.' One big hand gently stroked the hair back from her face. Then, when she said nothing, Lambis folded her closer, pushing her head against his chest, wrapping his arms around her.

'I was an idiot.' That hypnotic voice welled from deep within, vibrating beneath her ear. 'I didn't see until it was too late.'

'What didn't you see?' Amelie knew she should pull back and stand on her own two feet. She was a princess of St Galla, soon to be Regent, an independent, confident woman. But she couldn't bring herself to leave the shelter of Lambis's arms. It would be the last time he held her, surely, and she wasn't ready to miss a second of it. Later she'd berate herself for being weak and needy but not now.

His hand swept her back in a slow, soothing stroke. 'That I loved you.'

'What?' Her head jerked back and she found herself staring up into dark, serious eyes.

'I love you, Amelie.'

She shook her head, wondering why he'd torment her this way. 'You love your wife.'

'She and Dimitri will always hold a special place in my heart.' He spoke slowly, his tone measured as if to emphasise his meaning. 'But I've loved you for a long time. For years. Even when I rejected you here in St Galla, I loved you.'

Amelie strained back against his hold. 'No. You're saying that because you think it's what I want to hear. I don't need a husband, Lambis. I can get by without. Seb and I will be fine.'

'But I won't.' The words, so grave, so forthright, stopped her mid protest. 'I love you, Amelie, and I need you. I hadn't realised how much till I saw I was losing you.'

Bewildered, Amelie tried to make sense of his words. He looked at her with such openness, as if sharing such feelings was completely natural. Yet this man had deliberately isolated himself, protecting himself from emotions as far as he could.

'There's no need for this. I'm not marrying Alex. I'm not marrying anyone. Now, please, let me go.' She'd reached her limit. Standing in the circle of his arms, encompassed by his heat, feeling his heart beating beneath her hand, was too intimate.

Lambis closed his eyes and said something under his breath in Greek. Amelie couldn't understand a word, but felt his big frame shudder.

Then his eyes snapped open and it was like looking at a pewter sky, bright with sheet lightning. Slowly his mouth tipped into a wide smile, a grin that, despite her churning emotions, she couldn't help responding to.

'I think I loved you from the first day we met,' he said in that low, mesmerising voice. 'You were beautiful and kind and so utterly unaware of how entrancing you were.'

Amelie shook her head. 'You scowled at me.'

'I was a grouch. I was mired in guilt and regret and right from the start you made me feel things I didn't deserve to feel.'

Amelie's heart rolled over as she read the honesty in his eyes. Her hand slid up to his face, cupping that starkly angled jaw, feeling the erotic sensation of incipient bristles against her palm. 'You know you're not to blame. I hate that you feel like that and I'm sure Delia would hate it too.'

Unwavering, his eyes met hers and this time she read a flicker of assent there.

'You don't have to do this, Lambis. I'm really not going to marry Alex.'

'You think I'm lying?' His brow furrowed into a scowl that should have made him look forbidding yet only made her melt. 'I've been many things, Amelie, but no liar. I was brutally cruel when you came to me in Greece. I reneged on my duty to Sébastien because I was scared.' His deep breath pushed their chests together. 'I was scared of what you made me feel. Scared I'd be unfaithful to Delia's memory.'

Amelie nodded, trying and not quite succeeding in quashing a flare of jealousy.

'I didn't understand then.' Lambis brushed back a stray strand of hair from her face. 'Delia was my past. You're my present, Amelie, and my future. If you'll have me.' His voice shook. 'I love you, sweetheart. Would you consider marrying me?'

Yes. Say yes.

She tasted the word in her mouth.

'You only decided you cared when you saw me with Alex.' Pushing the words out took all Amelie's willpower. 'Because you thought I'd marry him.' She had to be sure.

Lambis shook his head. 'You're wrong. I knew when I made that appalling proposal a few hours ago. As soon as I blurted the words I realised it was what I wanted, but not for the reasons I told myself. It wasn't about protecting the pair of you. It wasn't about duty.'

His voice dropped to a rumbling bass pitch that reached her very core. 'I want to marry you for utterly selfish reasons. Because I love you. I need you. You turn my darkness into light. You give me a reason to wake each day. A reason to smile.' He lifted his hand and wiped the moisture that spilled down her cheek. 'You give me life, Amelie.'

She stared into that strong face, now vivid with hope and, could it be, love?

'At least give me a chance to show you how it can be between us. Given time you might come to love me too.'

There was such yearning in his voice, such intensity in those glittering grey eyes, Amelie felt the last of her defences crumble. 'I do love you, Lambis. I've loved you so long.'

She barely got the words out before his mouth was on hers, his arms crushing her to him. She felt the fine tremors racking his body, the hard, quickened pulse of his heart and dared, for the first time, to believe.

His kiss was a wonder. Not urgent like his embrace, but tender, so tender awe rose within her.

To be so loved, and by such a man. Was it possible?

When he lifted his mouth, he pressed kisses over her face and she caught a broken stream of Greek that, despite the language difference, made her heart swell. For they were unmistakably words of love.

Amelie cupped her hands around his face and drew it up so she could meet his eyes. They shone over-bright, in a way she'd never seen. 'I love you, Lambis Evangelos.'

'And I love you.' He paused, frowning. 'I don't even know your surname! Do royals even have surnames?'

Amelie stifled a laugh. 'They do. But I have a fancy to change mine.'

Instantly his hold tightened so much she had trouble drawing breath. But she didn't complain because the look on Lambis's face was one she'd never tire of.

'Could you bear to marry a commoner? A foreigner?'

'There's absolutely nothing common about you, my love. You're the light of my life.'

For long still moments they gazed into each other's eyes. 'Amelie Evangelos has a ring to it,' he said finally. 'If you're sure?'

'I've never been more sure of anything in my life.'

EPILOGUE

IT WAS A small wedding by royal standards, since Amelie and Lambis hadn't wanted to wait. Their eagerness had nothing to do with that last, unguarded morning in Greece when neither had thought about protection. Though more and more Lambis found himself speculating with excitement about the way his betrothed glowed.

Surveying today's crowd, he wondered how much more pomp and splendour a large royal wedding would manage.

The St Gallans had pulled out all stops for their beloved Princess. From the VIPs filling the great cathedral to the thousands gathered in the square outside, everyone wore finery, silks and jewels, dazzling uniforms or bright traditional cottons.

Flowers were everywhere. In huge arrangements and pinned to dresses and shirts, or carried ready to toss before the bride and groom as they left the cathedral.

Lambis swallowed, overcome by the familiar feeling that he didn't deserve this, didn't deserve Amelie. That he'd wake up and discover it a dream.

'Don't be scared, Lambis. I'll help you.' Beside him Sébastien's face was grave but his eyes sparkled. 'I know about important ceremonies.'

He did. Only a week ago he'd given his formal acceptance speech before parliament, on the same day Amelie had been made Regent.

'Thank you, Your Highness. I'm lucky to have you as my best man.'

The boy frowned. 'It's only Highness in public. *You* know that.' A small hand slipped into his. 'If you're scared, I'll hold your hand.'

Emotion blindsided Lambis as he looked down into those eyes so like his beloved Amelie's. It wasn't only Amelie he loved. The three of them were already a family. 'Thank you, Seb. I'd like that.'

A trumpet fanfare sounded high above and Lambis's heart quickened. Slowly he turned.

In the front row, with the new Prime Minister and other dignitaries, was Cat Dubois, eye-catching in green and almost as pretty as her half-sister. She smiled and winked. Beside her, King Alex of Bengaria looked ridiculously handsome in his dress uniform but his eyes were only for Cat, so Lambis had come to like his almost brother-in-law. Lambis's own friends were scattered in the front rows, either grinning at him or craning for a view of the bride.

The music changed to something softer yet jubilant and there was movement in the great arched doorway. Out of the light stepped two figures.

One, upright despite her years, was Lady Enide, beaming as Lambis had never seen her.

Holding her arm was Amelie. Gorgeous Amelie, who regularly stole his breath with just a smile. Now, wearing a long traditional gown, she was stunning. The fitted bodice of heirloom lace accentuated her slim yet lush femininity. The spreading skirt and the glimpse he caught of a delicate train made her look like something out of a fairy story. She wore no veil, but had been persuaded to wear a tiara of brilliant diamonds, trembling and glittering as she moved. She'd joked that wearing it might lessen their height difference at the altar.

All that Lambis took in with one sweeping glance before his eyes locked on hers. Heat pounded through him, and pride. The Princess Regent of St Galla was utterly magnificent, and she was his. He grinned and watched her mouth twitch into an answering smile.

Then she was before him and everything else faded.

'No second thoughts?' He held her gaze.

'Never,' she whispered.

'Good.' Against all protocol he bent and nuzzled her ear. 'Because I'm never letting you go.' He grazed her cheek with his lips and straightened, satisfied now her eyes shone brighter than her diamonds.

Then he closed his left hand around hers, his

right hand still grasping Sébastien's, and turned the three of them towards the waiting archbishop.

His love. His family. For ever.

* * * * *

If you enjoyed
THE GREEK'S FORBIDDEN PRINCESS,
don't miss the first part of Annie West's
THE PRINCESS SEDUCTIONS *duet*

HIS MAJESTY'S TEMPORARY BRIDE
Available now!

Get 2 Free Books,
Plus 2 Free Gifts—
just for trying the Reader Service!

HARLEQUIN *Romance*

YES! Please send me 2 FREE Harlequin® Romance LARGER PRINT novels and my 2 FREE gifts (gifts are worth about $10 retail). After receiving them, if I don't wish to receive any more books, I can return the shipping statement marked "cancel." If I don't cancel, I will receive 4 brand-new novels every month and be billed just $5.34 per book in the U.S. or $5.74 per book in Canada. That's a savings of at least 15% off the cover price! It's quite a bargain! Shipping and handling is just 50¢ per book in the U.S. and 75¢ per book in Canada.* I understand that accepting the 2 free books and gifts places me under no obligation to buy anything. I can always return a shipment and cancel at any time. The free books and gifts are mine to keep no matter what I decide.

119/319 HDN GLWP

Name	(PLEASE PRINT)
Address	Apt. #
City	State/Prov.	Zip/Postal Code

Signature (if under 18, a parent or guardian must sign)

Mail to the **Reader Service:**

IN U.S.A.: P.O. Box 1341, Buffalo, NY 14240-8531
IN CANADA: P.O. Box 603, Fort Erie, Ontario L2A 5X3

Want to try two free books from another line?
Call 1-800-873-8635 or visit www.ReaderService.com.

* Terms and prices subject to change without notice. Prices do not include applicable taxes. Sales tax applicable in N.Y. Canadian residents will be charged applicable taxes. Offer not valid in Quebec. This offer is limited to one order per household. Books received may not be as shown. Not valid for current subscribers to Harlequin Romance Larger-Print books. All orders subject to approval. Credit or debit balances in a customer's account(s) may be offset by any other outstanding balance owed by or to the customer. Please allow 4 to 6 weeks for delivery. Offer available while quantities last.

Your Privacy—The Reader Service is committed to protecting your privacy. Our Privacy Policy is available online at www.ReaderService.com or upon request from the Reader Service.

We make a portion of our mailing list available to reputable third parties that offer products we believe may interest you. If you prefer that we not exchange your name with third parties, or if you wish to clarify or modify your communication preferences, please visit us at www.ReaderService.com/consumerschoice or write to us at Reader Service Preference Service, P.O. Box 9062, Buffalo, NY 14240-9062. Include your complete name and address.

HRLP17R2

Get 2 Free Books,
Plus 2 Free Gifts—
just for trying the
Reader Service!

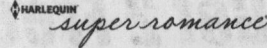

HSRLP17R

Get 2 Free Books,
Plus 2 Free Gifts—
just for trying the Reader Service!

HARLEQUIN
INTRIGUE

Get 2 Free Books,
Plus 2 Free Gifts—
just for trying the Reader Service!

HARLEQUIN®
MEDICAL ~Romance™